YPSILANTI
DISTRICT LIBRARY

37101930253516

ALSO BY IRINI SPANIDOU / *God's Snake*

WITHDRAWN

Fear

Irini Spanidou

Fear   A novel

WITHDRAWN

Alfred A. Knopf

New York

1998

Ypsilanti District Library
5577 Whittaker Rd.
Ypsilanti, MI 48197-9752

THIS IS A BORZOI BOOK
PUBLISHED BY ALFRED A. KNOPF, INC.

Copyright © 1998 by Irini Spanidou

All rights reserved under International and Pan-American Copyright Conventions.
Published in the United States by Alfred A. Knopf, Inc., New York, and
simultaneously in Canada by Random House of Canada Limited, Toronto.
Distributed by Random House, Inc., New York.

www.randomhouse.com

Grateful acknowledgment is made to Panther Music Corporation for
permission to reprint an excerpt from "The Great Pretender"
by Buck Ram, copyright © 1955 by Panther Music Corporation,
copyright renewed. International copyright secured.
Used by permission of Panther Music Corporation, c/o Peermusic.

Library of Congress Cataloging-in-Publication Data
Spanidou, Irini.
Fear : a novel / by Irini Spanidou. — 1st ed.
p.   cm.
ISBN 0-394-58055-9
I. Title.
PS3569.P354F43   1998
813'.54—dc21   98-14572
                                CIP

Manufactured in the United States of America
First Edition

WITHDRAWN

To the memory of my father,

PANAYOTIS C. SPANIDIS,

and for my mother,

NINA SPANIDOU

Fear

They called them "Saint John's fires," but they were of the ancient gods—a summer solstice ritual as close to myth and magic, and as old, as the cult of Demeter. Men, women, and children—little ones in their parents' arms—jumped through the flames, and as they jumped, they chanted, "I'm done with the bad; I'm new with the good." This was done three times. The first jump was one's strength, the second jump was one's courage, and the third jump was the jump that counted, for the third jump was one's luck. And while everyone else jumped, a young girl chosen by lot was sent to fetch spring water. She carried her pitcher to the fountain, then back home, and if perchance she met someone on the road, she kept silent and uttered no greeting or other word. For this was the "Unspoken Water." And when she got home, the girls who had jumped through the fire would be waiting for her, and they would throw their rings in the pitcher, and make a circle around her, and begin to sing. And she, who had been forbidden to jump through the fire—she, now forbidden to sing—would dip her hand in the pitcher and bring out a ring; and the words being sung the moment the ring passed the pitcher's rim would tell the owner's fortune. But for the girl holding the Unspoken Water, fate could not be foretold.

Two Days in June

SHE HAD JUST turned thirteen. Her name was Anna Karystinou and she was the daughter of an army colonel. On the evening this story begins, she was wearing a dress she had long outgrown. It was faded and frayed, fit her tightly at the bodice, squashing her breasts, and rode up her waist, drooping unevenly above her knees. She looked much older than her age, and the childish dress—with its puffed sleeves, round collar, and a belt that tied in a bow at the back—lent her an affronting innocence.

It was Saint John's Eve, June 1959. All day, this day of the solstice, there had been no sun. Now, with nightfall coming on, the sky was low, the color of charred steel. There was no wind. The bonfire in the middle of the street heaved upward with a steady, lapping quiver. A group of neighborhood children stood huddled nearby, waiting for the flames to become low enough to skim.

Anna stood apart at some distance. She had tried to meet the other children's eyes but had been shunned, and now, standing with legs slightly apart, a stiff back and arms straight at the sides like a sentry, she was staring steadfastly at the flames.

It was the moment in twilight when there are no shadows on the ground. For a while, the fire seemed to exist as in a

dream, a shadowless light of solitude. But when the darkness became deeper and the light of the fire brighter, it was
as if Anna had never seen fire before. She was filled with
awe, mesmerized as she watched. She was a good ten yards
away and yet, under the clammy coolness of her skin, she felt
flushes of heat, gentle, swelling, pulsing to the flames' quiv-
ering beat. Like the fire, she thought—burning unburned,
she was burning.

The other children, who had ignored her deliberately till
then, now began watching her intently. After a while, one of
them, a girl her age, broke away from the rest and walked
over. She was wearing a pink-on-white polka-dot dress with
a low-cut V neck and low-hung tapered waist, and she had
her hair in a ponytail tied with a wide pink ribbon. Her
features were irregular—wide mouth with a pouting lower
lip, snub nose, small recessed eyes—but as the aura of decay
makes a fall leaf splendid, an aura of ugliness made her face
beguilingly pretty. She was taller and slimmer than Anna,
pert in a winsome way, and carried herself with taut grace—
a vain, if somewhat shy, awareness of her appeal.

"Not one of the heathen?" she said in a contentious, sarcastic voice.

Anna gave her a startled glance. By the confusion in her
eyes, it was clear she had not taken in the meaning.

"Not one of the heathen?" the girl repeated. This time,
her voice was flat.

Comparing her own dress with the girl's, Anna was
ashamed. Blushing, she lowered her eyes. When she looked
up again, she was still red, but no emotion showed on her
face. She stared at the girl's chest, the darts that pointed to
her breasts, and started to say something, but the girl moved
away abruptly, ran to the fire, leapt over its flames, and

kept running. When she came to the end of the street, she stopped, turned around, gazed at Anna a moment, then slowly rounded the corner, glancing over her shoulder.

She had jumped over the fire when the flames were highest, when no one else dared, and Anna was amazed at the girl's nerve. Why had she walked up to her, why had she run away, and why had she looked back? It was like being jostled on a lifting swing, someone jerking one of the chains to see if you'd fall.

Unwittingly, deep in thought, Anna took a step back, and as she moved, she realized that the children were suddenly all looking at her again, with leers on their faces. She had had such confrontations before when moving into new territory. But in the small villages near outposts where she had lived year after year, the village children came out in force and besieged her. They may have shown hostile curiosity at first, staring at her silently in challenge, but in the end were quick enough to say the first word. In the week since she had lived on this street, these children had treated her with pointed indifference—the once-over dismissive glance that lingers just long enough to jab.

She began to walk backward with slow steps, her eyes level with theirs. They can have their fire, she thought. They can have their game.

Behind her, the street dead-ended in a churchyard. It was filled with aspen and cypress trees. The ground had been stepped smooth and hard, without a blade of grass, and gleamed in the darkness. The church was to the side, its belfry clearing the treetops, rising solitary, gray-white against the sky.

As she was reaching the churchyard, the wind started up. She could hear the leaves rustling and, distantly, the din of traffic, noises from the nearby streets. The city, unseen around her, seemed frightening, immense. She had the strange, unshakable sense that beyond its limits there was a void, that the world she once knew had ceased to exist. She had never felt this alone, this lonely.

The children were lining up to jump and the wind had started to gust, making the fire rage and slant. Anna watched the first boy take a leap, arms flailing, yelling at the top of his lungs as he straddled the flames. She wanted to join in. The sudden fury, the wild beauty of the flames were a burst of joy in her heart—a joy she was too frightened to let out, that tore like pain. She longed to run and leap. But her body was slack; her body was numb with fear.

AIMILIA KARYSTINOU, Anna's mother, was watching Saint John's fire from their living room window. Her frayed silk wrapper hung on her with wan elegance, its sheen dulled, its whiteness now gray. She was a beautiful woman, tall, lean, with a face that had no lines, no expressiveness except for a hint of anger in the eyes.

She thought of Saint John's fires in her own childhood, the girl she had been, the passion of joy pillaged from her. She dreaded dusk, dreaded the sudden stillness before darkness.

Leaning her forehead against the damp pane, she asked her second child, Maritsa, cuddled next to her, "Do you want to go down and jump over the fire?"

Maritsa shook her head no. She was a thin, pale five-year-old, with long legs and slightly hunched shoulders, her body stiff with shyness.

Aimilia picked her up and stood her on the sill. "All

right . . . all right," she said, moving to the other pane. "Stay with me."

The jumping had just come to an end, and the children had gathered near the diminishing fire. There was a blunt intensity in their gaze—a heightened, brooding emotion that merged their wills into one. Aimilia, feeling a tremor of foreboding, realized she had not seen her older daughter among the other children. Following their gaze, she saw Anna standing in the churchyard. Pigeons swarmed around her feet. She was standing next to a cypress tree—too close to it, too lax. It was unlike her to slump.

The church bell rang the vespers, and the pigeons fluttered their wings and flew up, scattering in the sky. Anna, startled, put her hand over her heart. Watching her, the other children laughed. It was a malicious, taunting laugh.

"Come on! Jump!" they shouted.

Anna began walking stiffly, as though in a trance. When she was three yards from the fire, she stopped. Her body started to shake; her knees buckled. She wobbled as if about to fall.

"Come on! Jump!" the children shouted again.

Their taunts became louder and louder.

"Jump! Jump! Jump!"

Aimilia had to hold herself back from shouting, too: Jump, idiot! Jump, fool! Anna was making a spectacle of herself. The fire, crumbling fast, was only two hand spans high. She could straddle it safely, would not even have to jump.

At last, she broke into a run, her body lurching forward as if she were about to tumble.

"Stop!" Aimilia screamed, flinging the window open. "Stop it!"

But Anna did not fall. She jolted to a stop just in front of the fire and stood still, her shoes touching the rim of the ashes, her skirt billowing over the flames.

The children had fallen silent while she was running. Now they began heckling her again. Two of the boys ran to the next yard and came back, carrying more junk wood and a cardboard box filled with packing straw. They threw them onto the flames and stepped back. The fire shot up, cinders popping high in the air. Anna did not move away, did not stir as the flames licked toward her face.

"Burn! Burn! Burn!" the children yelled.

Aimilia was too horrified at their cruelty to move, to speak.

"Daddy's come!" Maritsa said. "Look, it's Daddy!"

Stephanos Karystinos had just rounded the corner, his shadow shifting on the ground like a black searchlight. The children stopped yelling, turned to look, and, meeting his eyes, stood frozen. His face alert and stern, he walked on down the street with marching poise and pace. He did not have to look at them again. Slowly, they dispersed.

"It's Daddy!" Maritsa repeated.

"So it is," Aimilia said. Seeing Stephanos, she had felt a sudden cold creep over her. Her hands were like ice.

She went to sit down.

"Turn on the lights," she said to Maritsa.

"All the lights, Ma?"

"All the lights? All the lights?" she said, mimicking the child's voice. "What do I have to give for everything— detailed instructions?"

Maritsa turned the overhead lights on, then reached for the lamp switch on the end table and knocked down two framed photographs.

"All right! All right! I'll do it myself. God, let me have peace."

Maritsa backed up against the wall.

"Oh, stop looking like someone is about to kill you."

Aimilia straightened the pictures, placing them side by side. They were silver-framed studio portraits, one of herself, the other of Stephanos, taken two months before their wedding. She wore a strapless dress, a pearl choker around her neck. Stephanos was in dress military uniform. Neither of them was smiling.

Mother and daughter sat at opposite ends of the sofa, their legs uncrossed, hands on their laps. They did not look at each other or speak.

The room was high-ceilinged and large. There were no paintings, no ornaments anywhere. A Danish sofa with two end tables and three mismatched stuffed armchairs formed a circle. In the middle was an oblong coffee table with a wrought-iron base and a marble top. Under the blazing lights, against the glare of the empty white walls and bare wood floor, the sparse scuffed furniture, in its unabashed ugliness, evoked a desolate grandeur.

STEPHANOS CAME IN, followed immediately by Anna. Aimilia stared at them briefly, then looked away. Maritsa ran and tried to wrap her arms around Stephanos's knees, but he pushed her away.

"Anna!" he yelled at his other daughter.

Anna turned around and stood at attention. Her face was flushed from the heat of the fire, grimy with sweat and soot. She had the same features as Stephanos, the same coloring, the same intensity. They were bound by an instinctual understanding rather than by affection—an intimacy that was respectful but wary.

"Watch this." Stephanos lit a cigarette, put the lit end in his mouth, and then after a few seconds took it out. "It went out. The fire needs oxygen to burn."

He turned to Maritsa.

"Go get me a candle from the kitchen."

Maritsa ran to the kitchen and back. Stephanos took the candle from her, lit it, snuffed it with his fingers, lit it again.

"Snuff it," he said to Anna.

Anna stretched out her arm, held her hand steadily over the flame.

"Do it fast. So." He snapped his fingers.

She lowered her hand around the flame. More frightened of failing in his eyes than of being burned, she squeezed the wick slowly and winced, holding in the pain.

"It was your fear that burned you, not the flame. Understand?"

She turned her hand over and stared at her scorched fingers. "I understand."

"Go put some water on it," Aimilia said.

But Anna went straight into her room and slammed the door. They could hear her sob.

Stephanos turned to Aimilia.

"When are you going to put on a dress?" he said. "Before you go to bed?"

"Before we go out."

"You dress for me!" He took his military cap off. "We aren't going out. The car is in the shop."

Aimilia stared at the indentation, crimson and crinkled like a fresh scar, that the cap had left on his forehead.

"We could go to a taverna nearby," she said. "There's no food in the house."

"Fry some eggs."

"There's that nice place on the quay. . . ."

"I don't want to walk!" he said.

Aimilia looked away from him. It was one of the first things he had told her about himself. He did not like to walk. . . . When the army had disbanded after Greece's surrender to the Germans in 1941, he had walked with his men over mountainous terrain, in hunger, in thirst, in bitter cold, all the way down from the Albanian border. Going any distance on foot recalled that humiliation and defeat.

She had been moved when he first told her. It made her want to cry, how she had been moved then.

IT WAS A house of closed doors. One had to knock before entering a room, even a communal room. As at a barracks, however, no door, no closet, no drawer could be locked.

After hanging his cap in the hall, Stephanos walked to Anna's room and stood by the door, waiting for her to stop crying. When he could no longer hear her sobs, he paused an extra minute, then knocked.

"Who is it?" Her voice was angry.

Stephanos went in without answering.

She was standing in the dark. The only light in the room came through the open window from a lantern at the end of the street. As he closed the door behind him, the darkness deepened and her shadow stretched across the room to his feet like a rift.

"I was not afraid of getting burned," she said.

She turned on the small lamp by her bed, then faced him

with her arms crossed, squeezing her right hand into a fist. Her self-possession was daunting but misleading. She was blushing. She blushed easily, deeply. It made him worry—it made him fear for her—that she could not make her heart yield.

"I was not afraid of getting burned," she said again. "I was afraid of jumping."

Stephanos remembered being in the dark fuselage of a British plane with a parachute on his back. With him were other Greek officers who had fled to the Middle East after the Germans overran Greece and, forming the Sacred Band, had joined the Allied forces. They were infantrymen and had no paratrooper training. The man whose turn it was to jump held on to the gaping door frame and screamed, "I won't jump! I can't!" He backed down from the door and took his parachute off. The British CO gave orders to the next man in line. He jumped. And the next man. The next man. Stephanos's turn came. The Palestinian desert was purple-gray in the afterglow of the sunset. The beauty of the life-lessness, the total, flat emptiness below stunned him. He did not believe in God, yet, staring into the shimmering light, his knees shaking, he prayed for life. He was readying to leap when the man who had taken his parachute off thrust him aside. He had not put his parachute back on. It happened too fast—Stephanos had no time to react. When they found him, his body lay intact. There was no blood. For a moment, they thought he was still alive, but when they touched him, the flesh gave in like rubber. There were no solid bones left. It was like picking up a sack of wet sand.

Everyone had thought he had had a change of heart, that in his haste to redeem himself from disgrace he had forgotten that he had taken his parachute off. Perhaps. But there had been no rush of courage in the thrust of his arm. Stephanos had felt it on him, resolute, desperate. He had been afraid to jump, to risk life. He had not been afraid to die. It is the courage of the weak to welcome death, he thought, staring at his daughter. It is the power of the wounded to welcome pain.

He looked away from her.

"You don't believe me," Anna said.

"I believe you—that's what's bothering me."

He leaned against the wall and looked at her, trying to gauge from the tension in her face the severity of the burn.

"Show me your hand."

She loosened her fist but did not turn over her palm.

"My hand is fine," she told him.

He had made her willful, he realized. He had made her strong; he had made her proud. He had taught her diligently, methodically—he had given his all, trying to make her into a "real man." What had he known of her soul? What did he know, now, of the changes beginning in her body? Earlier, by the fire's light, he had seen her naked through her dress—her breasts, the slope of her waist, the cleft between her legs. In this muted light, as she bent her right leg, raising the heel and resting it against her left ankle, as she slanted her head and stared at him, her beauty, stealthy with innocence, aroused him.

"You're becoming a woman," he said, shaking his head.

Sorrow suffused his face, so profound, it blotted out his features. When he had first held her, her swaddled body like a bundle of rags, her infant face so like his own, the sense of her life merging with his had seemed a bestowal of grace. Now he felt like a man shipwrecked, with nothing to keep him afloat but the dread of drowning.

THE NEXT MORNING, Aimilia woke up early. It was still dark, a misty dawn light. Stephanos lay on his back next to her, snoring. She was too tense to go back to sleep. She got up, made a cup of coffee, then sat out on the porch and drank it as the sky changed to pink, to a hazy blue. A cold breeze, coming in from the sea, made the apple tree by the porch railing sway. The two swallows that nested in the eaves swooped low over the roses and flew away. It was going to rain again.

Beyond the garden and the next two streets rose a range of hills, the Upper City creeping up its slopes. There was a distant din of traffic and, closer, the cries of itinerant merchants beginning to sell their wares. Thessaloniki was slowly coming to life.

In the garden of her home in Egypt, the swelling Nile, calm, majestic, flowed beyond the fence; palm trees and bougainvillea vines shimmered in the morning dew under a pale blue sky; smoldering air melted the skin. The dense, numbing light instilled languor, faith in fatalism, a mystical existence. Her life had once had the soothing weight of dreams, a beauty inexorable and austere. Greek light made each tree, each leaf, each rock, each crevice in the parched ground shine hard-edged, separate. It forced you into yourself, a ruthless solitude. You could see it in the fierce-staring depth—the seething darkness in people's eyes. You could see it in her own eyes now. The sap came from the soil, not the root. The transplanted tree adapted or withered.

She had lived in more than a dozen towns, more than a dozen houses since her marriage to an army man. They moved and moved. And lived the same life. New houses, different houses, filled with the same things.

The seat of the chair was damp and her backside was getting cold, but she did not want to go back inside. She could hear Stephanos on his way to the bath, then milling in the kitchen as he made coffee, each sound predictable and jarring, like the irregular ticking of a clock.

He came out, bringing his own coffee and a fresh cup for her. He had just shaved and had a bleeding cut above his lip.

She gave him her napkin to dab the blood. "It will rain—the birds were flying low," she said.

"Not till later."

"No."

They drank their coffee in silence—he in quick gulps, she sipping slowly. As soon as he was done, he went back into the house. She was cold but did not follow him inside. When she heard the front door slam, she got up, stretched, and, leaving the empty cups behind, went in.

The children were in the kitchen. Anna was making cocoa on the stove. Dry tear tracks meandered over the sooty grime on her cheeks. Maritsa was sitting on the table.

"Sit down on a chair like a human being," Aimilia said to her.

She turned to Anna. "Look at you," she said. "You're still covered with soot. Go take a shower—and use hot water."

Normally, Anna was not allowed to bathe with hot water. Cold showers, summer and winter, were part of the regimen Stephanos had devised for her. He allowed Aimilia no say in her upbringing. His pride—*his* daughter. "My new, revised edition" was how he liked to introduce her. It turned Aimilia's stomach.

"Do you hear anything I say?" she asked. "You could at least look at me when I speak."

Anna did not turn from the stove.

"Your father wants you to have a new dress. We'll go shopping after breakfast."

"Father?" Anna said, putting the cocoa on the table. "Father wants me to have a new dress?"

Aimilia could see she was pleased but that she did not want to let it show. She watched her pour the cocoa into Maritsa's cup, then take the empty saucepan to the sink.

"I had a strange dream last night," Anna said, coming back to the table. "I dreamt of the moon."

"The moon?" Aimilia said absently. "What about the moon?"

Anna did not answer.

Aimilia went to her room, took her lavender linen suit out of the closet, set it on the bed, and rummaged in the top drawer of the bureau for stockings. She found a light beige pair, slid her hand in and out. There was a pulled thread in the back. Stretched on her leg, it would run. There was no other light-colored pair. She would have to wear a deeper shade and the color would look all wrong. It was enough to ruin her day.

When she got dressed, however, it did not look so bad. The dark stockings blended nicely with her tan.

"Anna!" she called out. "Anna! Are you ready?"

Anna came to the door. She had washed her hair and had put on a striped chemise dress, a hand-me-down of Aimilia's. The hem had been raised, but the rest of the dress had not been altered. The stripes were too wide for her height, and the short sleeves and collar gaped.

"Your belt is tied too tight," Aimilia told her. "Loosen it!"

Anna slipped a finger in and out of the belt. "It isn't."

"Loosen it! It makes you look like a wasp."

"I like it this way."

"Well, you look ridiculous. Go see if Mr. Marketou will keep an eye on Maritsa while we're gone."

Mr. Marketou was the Karystinous' elderly landlord, who lived upstairs with his wife. They had no children of their own and had taken a wistful liking to Maritsa.

Anna headed for the front door.

"He's out back," Aimilia said. "I just saw him come down."

Anna came to a halt and turned around with barely controlled fury. She had always been unmanageable with her mother, but during the last few months she had begun to react to Aimilia's commands with a violence that approached hatred.

When she came back, she had tied her belt even tighter and had unfastened the two top buttons of her dress so that the bulge of her breasts and a bit of bra lace showed through. Aimilia decided to let it go. But then, as though daring her, Anna spit on her fingers and twisted the hair above her ears onto her temples.

Aimilia closed her eyes and pressed her thumb and fingers against her forehead.

"Anna," she said, "you have a nice face, a nice body. Trust me—I'm your mother. It doesn't become you, what you're trying to do. It makes you look vulgar."

She leaned over, brushed the hair off her daughter's face, and tried to button up her dress.

"Can we go?" Anna said, pushing her away.

Aimilia stopped at the mirror in the hall to check her lipstick. The shoulder seams of her jacket were at a slight slant. She straightened them and rearranged the folds of her scarf.

"Can we go!" Anna said. She had opened the door and was standing just outside the landing.

They walked to the bus stop in silence, without looking at each other.

AGAIN AND AGAIN, Anna thought of her dream. It had been strange and unsettling—air drained of light, darkness like mist stretching infinitely around her. She was standing on muddy ground, a fresh grave at her feet, and as she looked down, she saw that its bottom was filled with water—a black murky gleam. Floating in it, as though drowned, was the swollen face of the moon. It had the sullen pallor and severity of new life, like the face of a newborn before it has begun to breathe.

"Here, right on this spot, you first struck out on your own," Aimilia said as they got off the bus. "We've lived here before, you know. Must have been when you were two and a half, three years old.

"I had been arguing with your father, and I let go of your hand. You walked by yourself to the intersection, then backed off the curb, afraid to cross. 'Let's wait and see what she does,' your father said. 'Let's let her panic. It will teach her a lesson not to walk off alone.'

"You knew enough not to cross traffic. When we caught up with you, you said, 'Why don't streets have bridges?' "

Anna did not remember the incident, but she remembered another time, when she was a little older—perhaps four. They were in Athens, in one of the busiest sections of town, near Omónia Square. It was during the evening rush hour. She remembered it being dark—throngs of people rushing to the bus depot. Her parents were having an argument this time as well, but it had been her father holding her hand, her father who had let her go. She was carried away by the crowd—pushed and jostled between people's legs. She started sobbing—howling with terror. Stephanos caught up with her, grabbed her shoulders, and shook her, shouting, "Why are you bawling? Who's allowed you to bawl? If you're ever lost again, what you'll do is go find a policeman and tell him you're lost."

She had thought what he meant was that she should give herself up to the policeman—surrender for the crime of being lost.

"I don't remember. I don't remember at all," Aimilia said after Anna had recounted her memory. "I can see we were cruel. We were too young. People should not have children when they're too young. They're too selfish."

She was walking faster than Anna, speaking in a toneless voice, as though to herself.

"I was a child myself when I had you. I was more of a child then than you are at your age now. I had grown up spoiled, too sheltered."

Anna had heard it all before. She wanted to be in the

store, to get it over with, to go home. But when they were actually in the store, she became excited. It turned out that she was too big for children's clothes and they had to go to the women's section.

The saleswoman who came out to help them was older, with dyed black hair slicked down with brilliantine. She wore poppy red lipstick and had penciled in her eyebrows with an unsteady hand.

"A dress for the young miss?" she said.

Anna blushed. It was the first time anyone had called her "miss."

"Something simple—in cotton," Aimilia said curtly.

The saleswoman brought out a single dress from the racks and displayed it for them.

"But that's *my* size!" Aimilia said.

"It's mercerized cotton, imported from France," the saleswoman said in a surly manner.

It was fuchsia-pink, with a scooped neck and no sleeves. Its only ornament was the discreet lace piping along the seams. Anna looked at it with disappointment. She had wished for something flamboyant, with ruffles and frills.

"I'll try it," she said.

When she put the dress on in the fitting room, she was amazed to see that it fit snugly, like a sweater, forming a clear delineation of her breasts, waist, and hips, as if she were naked underneath. It made her look like a full-grown woman. It made her look . . . stupendous. That was the word for it—*stupendous!* She looked so beautiful, it was impossible to believe. And yet it was as if she had always known she could look like this—*would* look like this.

She ran out of the dressing room to show her mother.

"It makes you look too old," Aimilia said.

"It happens, doesn't it—just like that," the saleswoman said. "Next you'll see her in a wedding dress and won't know where the time went."

"We could do without the commentary," Aimilia said under her breath. She went closer to Anna and whispered, "I don't think it's a practical dress. You couldn't wear it to play. I don't know *where* you'd wear it."

"Mama, it's so beautiful!"

"It's too tight."

"Tight! It makes her look luscious," the saleswoman said. "She's enough to make a priest sin."

Aimilia winced.

"We were looking for an everyday dress," she said. "What else do you have?"

"Oh, Mama! I want it!"

"You can't have it. Let's not make a scene."

Anna raised her arms and twirled.

"Mama, look!" she said pleadingly. "It makes me a different person."

"She stained the armpits!" the saleswoman said.

Anna looked down at herself. There were indeed wide wet stains.

"You will have to buy it now," the saleswoman said, smirking.

Other people in the store were staring.

"Madam—" Aimilia began.

"There's no argument," the saleswoman said firmly. "We can't sell a stained dress."

Aimilia asked the price. It was over the amount Stephanos had given her, but they had her under the gun, and she knew she couldn't bargain. She added some of her own money, put it on the counter, and walked out of the store, pulling Anna along.

"Mama, I haven't changed back. My old dress is in the store."

"We're not going back there ever—for anything."

They rushed on down the street.

"Wait till your father sees that I bought you a party dress when you have nothing decent to wear," Aimilia said. She burst out laughing, sobbing with hysterical laughter. "Wait till your father sees."

She was laughing so hard she had to double over.

"Let's go someplace and have a snack," she said, trying to catch her breath. "When I splurge, I splurge."

They walked into the first café they found. It turned out to be a nice place, with wooden tables and leather-upholstered chairs. There were only two other customers—two elderly solitary men, sitting at separate tables. They raised their eyes when Aimilia and Anna walked in, then went back to reading their morning papers.

A considerable time after Aimilia and Anna sat down, a waiter approached. He was a middle-aged man, bald, with a pencil-thin mustache and flabby jowls. He bent over, his hands behind his back, and said in an obsequious voice, "What would you like to order?"

"Two cheese pies, one coffee medium-sweet, one lemonade," Aimilia said.

"I want ice cream, Mama," Anna protested.

"Certainly not. It's before lunch."

"God help us!" the waiter said. "Can the young woman be your daughter, ma'am?"

He looked genuinely astonished.

"Two cheese pies, one coffee medium-sweet, one lemonade," Aimilia repeated.

"I don't want you to call me Mama in public from now on," she said to Anna. "Don't you see? I'm too young to be your mother."

Anna did not answer.

The waiter brought their food and they ate in silence.

"We are like sisters, you and I," Aimilia said when she was done eating. There was a beseeching softness in her eyes. "It's friends that we should be—best friends."

Her mother could not be a friend, Anna thought. Her mother was her mother. But she had never seen Aimilia's face look so soft, her beauty no longer a cold, imperious glow, but come to life—atremble with gentleness, with loneliness, with want. Anna felt an overwhelming sudden love, then unease. She sensed her mother's unhappiness; she sensed her mother's fear. She is alone, she thought. Her life is as separate from others as my own.

"As friends do," Aimilia said, "I'll tell you a secret. My name is not Aimilia. I was christened Eulalia, after my father's mother. When I was five or six, I told everyone my name would be Aimilia from that day on, and I refused to answer when they called me by my real name."

"Why?"

"Eu-*lal*-ia? Some prissy spinster might fit the name. You can't seriously think *I* could be a Eulalia?" Aimilia said. And when Anna did not answer, she said, "You tell me a secret. Your turn."

"I don't have any secrets."

"I'm thinking, you know," Aimilia said. "I'm thinking how upset I was when I found out I was pregnant with you—how miserable. I remember crying like a child. 'I don't want

it! I won't have it!' I screamed, and our landlady at the time
—an old peasant woman—asked, 'And what do you aim to
do—digest it? It will come out, my daughter, from whence it
came in, and that's God's wish and not for us to say. Too late
to cry now and too early. Save your cries for birthing.'

"I will die, I thought. Two days and nights I was in labor.
I shouted the house down—kept the whole neighborhood
awake. You tore me clean through when you came. Four people had to hold me down when they sewed me, and that was
the next day, for there had been no doctor nearby."

There was excitement in her voice, the animation one
brings to the telling of a gripping story. The absence of any
underlying pain or regret made the facts both more vivid
and less real. Anna could not picture her birth, yet she was
horrified.

"When they brought you to me to nurse, my breasts were
so sore that they bled. You drank my blood together with
your milk, did you know? Now you're suddenly grown. Now
I've got myself a friend—the sister I never had. Who would
have thought!"

Anna lowered her eyes. Ever since she could remember,
her mother's naked breasts had made her heart flutter with an
emotion there was no single name for. It was joy; it was
dread; it was love that made the tongue swell. On being told
she had mauled them suckling, her stomach cramped and her
mouth filled with a rusty acrid-sweet taste, as though she'd
brought up the old blood. She was sick.

"So, we're friends?" Aimilia said. "Look at me!"

When Anna would not look up, Aimilia took hold of her
hand, then let it go abruptly.

"Your hand is cold! Are you cold?"

Anna shook her head. "It's about to rain," she said. "We should go."

Aimilia looked out the window.

"I guess we should. Let's walk; I feel like walking. It's not going to rain yet."

They started to walk home. Anna kept silent. She walked fast, her head down.

"What's come over you? What's wrong?" Aimilia asked.

"Nothing's wrong. I want to get home."

"What's there to do at home that won't wait?"

"I want to read my book."

"You want to read your book!"

They made it home just as the rain started. Anna went to the kitchen, looking for something to eat. She wanted something sweet, mushy. There was leftover cake on the counter, but it looked dried-out. The only food in the icebox were the stuffed peppers from the day before, which had been inedible. Instead of sweet red peppers, Aimilia had used hot ones by mistake. One small bite made the inside of the mouth feel as though skinned and salved with iodine.

"We forgot to shop for lunch," Aimilia said, coming into the kitchen.

Anna stood with her hand on the open icebox door and stared at the pot on the mold-covered shelf.

"What are you saving this for?" she said with exasperation. "What are you *saving* it for!"

"I don't have the heart to throw it out. I made it."

The earlier softness was completely gone from her face. She looked at Anna the way she always did when looking at her directly—eyes sullen and slightly unfocused, as though startled by some unwelcome thought.

"Go take off your dress," she said. "You don't want to stretch it out of shape. Make sure to hang it on a padded hanger. Take one from my closet."

Anna went to her parents' room to get the hanger. The mirror on the armoire door was marbled with rust, swirls of gray shadow spreading like seepage from the beveled edges. She could not see her reflection clearly.

She went to her room and changed into shorts and a T-shirt. There was no mirror in her room. But though there was no way for her to see herself, she had the sense she looked just as she had wearing the dress. There was the same exhilarating sensation of a miraculous force—greater, more wonderful than life—pushing out from deep inside and forming a new delineation of her body, like a second, immaterial skin. It made her feel all-powerful—invincible. Standing by her bed, she cupped her hands over her breasts and pressed them hard as when something hurt and she wanted to stanch the pain. But it was pleasure she felt—a pleasure so deep, it took her breath away.

STEPHANOS CAME HOME for lunch and found the house empty. He had been caught in the rain and his shoes sloshed, spilling out water. He was soaked. As he hung up his hat, the back door creaked open and Maritsa came running in.

"Mama!" she called out. "Mama!" She looked startled to see him. "It's you, Daddy!"

She stared at his drenched uniform, the mud tracks he'd made, and she walked toward him with slow, hesitant steps.

"Hard rain," he said.

She followed him around the house—from the bedroom, where he changed, to the bathroom, where he hung his uniform to dry, to the living room.

"All right," he said. "What do you want?"

"Mrs. Marketou asked me to stay for lunch," she said, pressing against his legs. "May I? She's making mashed potatoes."

"You may."

She continued standing by his chair, staring at him.

"Oh, get up here!"

He lifted her onto his knees, but she moved to the edge of his thigh, sitting cautiously, as though on a high ledge.

"Mr. Marketou has a bullet in his head," she said. "Did

you know that, Daddy? The doctor can't get it out and it gives him a headache. Only when it rains. Were you wounded in the war, Daddy?"

There had been icy snow on the ground, and the sight of his spilled blood, bright red on white, staggered him with surprise. He felt no pain at first, watched as his blood kept flowing, splattering on the ice. Next to him, a corporal lay facedown. He nudged him, and he was alive. They helped each other up. There was a small stain of blood on the corporal's midriff, whereas Stephanos's whole chest was wet. "Lean on me, Lieutenant, sir," the corporal said. *Lean on me*. In the medics' tent, they were put side by side. A strong wind kept blowing the door flaps open. Through a gust, he saw snowflakes fall onto the corporal's open eyes. Death's icy tears melted and trickled down his cheeks.

"No . . ." he said.

He caressed her back, tenderness stirring slowly inside him.

"I'm going," she said. "Will you tell Mama where I am?"

"I'll tell her."

He watched her mince away. As soon as she was out of his sight, he could hear her break into a run.

He lit a cigarette but soon put it out. His underwear was damp, making him uncomfortable. He went to the bedroom, removed his clothes again, and lay down.

He had been transferred to Thessaloniki to attend War College. For the first time since he had seen active duty, he was stripped of the command of men, and had to sit at a desk—a pupil raising his hand. His classmates were career functionaries, paragons of the bureaucratic mind that ultimately runs an army. Theories about strategy . . . theories about weapons . . . he thought. Do you have it in you to look a man in the eye and say, "Go die"? That's what vocation for the military hinged on.

He was thirty-nine, and it had taken him until now to see through the illusions of youth. He was just beginning to realize what no school will teach you: Power cannot rest on heroes. Not because it corrupts, but because the true hero knows himself to be a means to a greater end than his own gain. It's selfish ambition that carries the day. Most heroes die unknown. He had seen hundreds of men fall at the front, and he had gone on fighting, averting his eyes. How could one look on and live? How could one remember and live? Worse than defeat, victory sullies. Those who survive usurp their lives.

He had never before experienced lassitude, bitterness, or self-doubt. During the war, to get through, he had to say day after day, night after night, "If I must die, I must. . . . If I must die, I must"—the silent repetition a truce between terror and reason. Now he was repeating it again. If I must die, I must. . . . If dreams must die, they must; if desires must die, they must; if hopes must die, they must.

He heard Aimilia and Anna come home. They went into the kitchen. He could hear their voices, the clatter of cupboard doors opening and closing.

"What's the matter?" Aimilia said, coming into the bedroom. "Are you sick?"

"No."

"Don't you want to eat?"

"No."

She went out. When she came back a few minutes later, Stephanos had his eyes closed.

"Are you still awake?"

"Yes."

She walked to the foot of the bed and let down her hair, taking the pins out one by one and holding them absently in her hand.

"Maritsa is with the Marketous—upstairs," he said. "They'll feed her."

She shook her head to unravel her hair and tossed the pins on top of the bureau. They scattered, most of them falling on the floor. She did not attempt to pick them up.

Her messiness was subverted aggression against him. How often had he asked her to be neat? She thwarted him, as though his need for order—for harmony—were a selfish whim.

She undid her blouse, pushed it off her shoulders, let it fall. She took off her skirt, underpants, bra—flaunted her nakedness like a royal flush.

"Would you throw me my nightgown?"

He pulled the nightgown from under the pillow and held it so that she had to come and get it.

She slipped it on, lay next to him, and, turning on her side, wormed her hand under his T-shirt.

"You're cold," she said. "You're wet. You've gotten the sheets wet!"

She pulled away and lay on her back.

Stephanos felt a paralyzing weariness, so sudden and extreme he thought he was going to black out. He tensed up, but there was no fight in him. He surrendered to sudden deep sleep. Four hours later, he woke up disoriented, limbs heavy and slack, as if he were running a fever. He had dreamt he was walking in a field. The grass was green and waved tranquilly like a billowing sea. The field was empty at first, but as he walked on, it became filled with men. They lay on their backs, their hands crossed over their genitals. He walked by each one. They all had the same face. They were all the same man.

It took all his strength to push himself up and sit at the edge of the mattress. It was seven o'clock. He had to pick up the car at the garage. He had to take Anna for a ride, spend time with her. He had to get moving.

"Anna," he shouted. "Come here!"

Anna walked in, carrying a book, with her forefinger inside the pages so she wouldn't lose her place. It was called *Alms for the Soul, a Few Crumbs of Wisdom*. Stephanos could not suppress a sneer, but it pained him: She read with a scavenger's avid greed anything she could get.

"I want to take you out," he said.

"Should I change?"

He stared at her and shook his head no. She looked like jailbait, her body in shorts and a tight tucked-in T-shirt making a mockery out of her earnest face. After the flood, try to shore up the banks of the river! he thought. She was out of his hands. Gone.

IT WAS A torrid evening. Despite the earlier downpour, the humidity, briny with vapors from the sea, was thick, stuck to the skin. In the taxi, the breeze from the open windows had cooled her down, but now, as she followed Stephanos into the garage, Anna felt sweat rolling down her calves from the hollows behind her knees. Her T-shirt was damp, a diaphanous stain spreading below the neckline to her breasts.

Except for an insistent sound of metal scraping on metal, the garage seemed empty. It was a small place and the smell of gasoline and oil was overpowering. The electric light had a yellow density like light in a cellar, but it was dim and

Anna had trouble adjusting her eyes. At last, she spotted the mechanic under a pickup truck. His legs stuck out and one of his feet twitched to the motion of his working arm. There was a hole in the sole of his shoe—widening uneven circles through layers of leather and, in the middle, a gleam of calloused skin. She looked away.

"Nico!" Stephanos said.

The mechanic did not respond.

"Nico!" Stephanos repeated irritably.

The mechanic rolled on his side and spit.

"Be right there."

Anna decided to wait outside. She was halfway to the door when she sensed she was being stared at. She turned abruptly. The mechanic had crawled from under the car and was standing in a taunting slouch, legs apart, head to the side. Like Anna, he was drenched in sweat. As she met his eyes, his pupils darkened, blurring with a sullen softness. She felt a strange, exciting liking for him—too thrilling, too sudden not to show on her face—and lowered her eyes. She was ashamed to like him—to have her father watching. She was sure he despised the mechanic: so unlike him, so beneath him—lax and surly at once, as though all it took to be a man was to stand up. She blushed horribly.

Stephanos stepped in front of her, standing with his back to her.

"Is my car ready?" he said.

The mechanic pushed the tip of his shoe in and out of a small puddle of oil. "It's ready. . . ." he said, dragging his voice. He lit a cigarette and, as he blew out the match, bent his head to the side and stared at Anna again.

"Go wait outside," Stephanos told her.

His voice was low and harsh, and Anna blushed again.

She went out and stood by the door. The street was unusually wide, to allow for heavy trucks, but now it was empty of traffic, strewn with refuse and discarded crates. In the deepening dusk, everything shimmered with the asphalt's gray, as if darkness were coming up from the ground, from inside the earth. Workers from nearby warehouses were leaving for home, walking with a slow, careworn gait, some lingering to smoke. They stared at her with the same gleaming darkness that had been in the mechanic's eyes, but harshly, the way someone looks at a person he wants to insult but haughtily holds back. The mechanic, too, had had an affronting leer on his face, but there was something else to it—something underneath that made her long to touch him. Thinking of him made her ashamed, anxious.

When Stephanos brought out the car, she crawled in fast, wanting to hide from view.

Stephanos jerked the car into gear.

"A man looks at you, you don't look back," he said. "A man looks at you—hear me?—you don't notice."

It was as if he had slapped her. She slid to the side of her seat, trying to sit as far away from him as she could, and looked out the window to distract her mind. She did not have a unified impression of Thessaloniki yet. She was beginning to recognize some streets by looks and name, but their strangeness was still jarring. In the avenue along the promenade and close to the harbor, the buildings were tall and new, a uniform unweathered white, and had a similar design of flat roofs, square windows, and railed balconies. Up the hill, the buildings were small, colored like yellowed ivory, with swollen walls that made them look slightly convex, molded into the ground as though made of the same clay. They were dispersed around relics from ancient Greek, Roman,

Byzantine, and Ottoman times, the past merging indistin-
guishably with the present. Yet here, too, on wider main
streets, there was a scattering of new, tall buildings. Some
store signs had stenciled block-letter inscriptions, some were
hand-painted in the painter's unique flourished script and
bore illustrative drawings, like store signs in villages.

"Where are we going?"

He did not answer her, and his silence, the way he drove,
staring straight ahead and pointedly ignoring her presence,
were beginning to scare her. They were driving uphill, out of
the city.

Along the highway, there was a drop at the shoulder of
the road. Below the cliff stretched a gentler slope, then the
descending hills, the waterfront's level flatness, the silver
glimmer of the sea. A mass of thick clouds hung over the
mountain, but the rest of the sky was clear. Lights were
beginning to come on—in scattered houses, on commercial
avenues, on the masts of ships anchored in the outer reaches
of the harbor.

The road was becoming more and more narrowly
twisted. Stephanos was driving at full throttle.

From age six to nine, Anna had lived with her grandparents because the bases where Stephanos had been sta-
tioned were too far from schools. When she went back to live
with her parents, she suffered attacks of vertigo—mostly in
the car, when Stephanos drove too fast. Stephanos never
commented or tried to ease her suffering by slowing down.
He would stop the car five, seven times a trip so she could get
out and vomit. She was too nauseated to stand up when she
got out, and she had to crawl out of the car, vomiting on her
hands and knees like a dog. Each time she got back in the car,

she thought with terror, We could fly off the cliff. . . . We could fly off the cliff. . . . One day—after several months— the fear became certainty. We're going to fly off, she thought. It no longer seemed to matter: She no longer vomited.

As he had not commented those times when she had asked him to stop the car, Stephanos did not comment the first time she went through a trip without asking. He let Aimilia and Maritsa out at the house, told Anna to get in front, and raced back up the hill. When they came to the top, he stopped the car and asked her to get out. They were at the edge of the road, the drop of a cliff. He let her stand a moment alone, then put his arm around her shoulder.

"I knew you'd come through," he said. "I knew you had it in you."

Now, as he sped up, for the first time in years the nausea came back. It was not strong enough to make her want to vomit, but she was sick with fear, sick with despair and shame. She didn't "have it in her"—never would. All that had happened was her fear had hidden to lie in wait more treacherously.

At last, they turned onto a gravel road. At the end was a secluded restaurant surrounded by thick shrubbery and pine. Red neon lights spelled PANORAMA across the roof. Stephanos and Anna walked through the building and out to the terrace in back.

There was a bandstand, a large dance floor, more than a hundred tables. Stringed lights in a radial pattern, starting at the roof of the bandstand and ending at poles at the end of the terrace, hung overhead. They were still unlit. A solitary waiter was spreading white linen cloths over the tables, securing them with clips against the wind, even though it was calm at present. A strong scent of wet earth, pine resin, and burned grease suffused the air. From somewhere inside came the discordant, strident sounds of a violin being tuned.

There were no other customers yet. Anna walked to the end of the terrace and leaned on the stone ledge. Stephanos stood a few steps back.

"It's like having the world at your feet," she said.

Stephanos wondered if she remembered the first time he had brought her here. She could not have been more than three. The place was just a modest bar and grill then, with bare wooden tables and stacks of wine barrels. The owner had a dog, and the dog was tied to a tree on the roadside. It growled viciously at them, then started barking. The owner shouted from the door, "Don't go near him! He'll bite." Instead of heeding the warning, she let go of Stephanos's hand and walked closer.

"You heard what the man said," he told her. "Get away or he'll bite."

The dog was pulling at his chain, and she stood about one foot away.

"Why will he bite?" she asked.

"Because he does not know you."

"I'm Anna Karystinou," she said to the dog. "An-na."

The trust and goodness of her innocence contained no fear. She kept repeating her name slowly, gently, and after awhile, the dog retreated near the tree. She took a step forward, another, stretching out her arm. There was no knowing if the dog might or might not attack. Stephanos ran to her, terrified, grabbed her, and slapped her on her back. He hit her again and again.

"I told you to stay away!"

She did not try to shield herself.

"Will you listen to me next time?"

"Yes."

"Will you listen?"

"Yes."

It was the first time he had hit her—the first time he had seen fear in her eyes, and the fear was of him. Fear of his own fear—to lose her, to have her come to harm.

"What's that?" she said now.

He walked to the ledge and looked down. There was a clearing of about fifty yards, then the woods of the ravine began. Just before the ground dropped, there was a mound of cut flowers, gathered in bouquets and wreaths.

"Someone must have died there," he said.

"Died *there?*" She was astonished. "How?"

"Must have been killed."

The waiter came over and stood behind them.

"That's where she breathed her last," he said. "She wasn't killed there. She was attacked back in the woods, the killer leaving her for dead, but she crawled her way out. They followed the trail of blood a hundred yards down the gorge."

"Who was she?" Anna asked.

"A woman . . . Nineteen years old, they say."

"Who killed her?"

"Same man who killed the other one," the waiter said.

"What other one?" Anna asked.

"There was another one found in the woods a month ago," the waiter said. "Her head bashed in with a stone—same as this one."

Anna lifted herself onto the ledge and sat down.

Stephanos and the waiter stared over her head down to the spot where the young woman had died. The sun had set and the horizon was fiery red, the ground deep purple. The flowers had been squashed by the midday rain and were crumbling, strewn with mud.

"The police believe it's someone who kills randomly," the waiter said.

Anna turned around and got off the ledge.

"Why?" she asked Stephanos. "Why would someone kill a stranger?"

The waiter walked to a table two yards away and unfolded the last tablecloth, shaking it out with a lashing motion.

Anna asked again, "Why would a man kill a stranger?"

"Not just a stranger," Stephanos told her. "A woman."

"Why would a man kill a woman?"

"Because she's a woman."

She did not understand. That he did understand, that his knowledge was unflinching, made her recoil. She turned her back to him and looked out across the gorge, at the unbounded expanse of the city and bay once again. Darkness had fallen. The sea was as black as the sky, and the small glittering lights looked puny—each solitary, each like a drop of molten wax.

Three Days in September

THE SCHOOL BUILDING was two stories high, wide and long, with an unadorned pediment roof and large elongated windows in austere symmetry to its shape. Wide marble steps led to an entrance with a Doric entablature and columns around the door. Anna was unnerved by its size but welcomed its imposing appearance. Beyond her greatest expectations, it made the occasion momentous. It *should* be indomitable and awesome, she thought. It was the portal to adult life.

She followed Aimilia up the steps.

It was registration day, but the whole place seemed deserted. They wandered through long, dark corridors and came to a cavernous hall with a stairway leading up. Despite the high ceilings and abundance of space, the effect was dreary and oppressive. The floor was covered with gray tiles; the walls had a coarse surface, a color and texture like the rough side of an oyster shell; the air was stale, smelled of mold and wet dust.

"You'd think there'd be a sign," Aimilia said.

"Is this the right day?" Anna asked.

Aimilia did not answer her, just said in a snappish tone, "Run out and ask the custodian for directions."

Anna went back out, deliberately dragging her steps.

The gatehouse was a small lean-to adjacent to the yard gate. The custodian, an old man with a deeply lined, placid face, sat on a stool, reading the paper. He glanced up when he heard Anna approach, but before she had a chance to speak, he returned to the paper and went on reading.

Anna surveyed the yard. It was bare—hard-packed earth, swept clean. The enclosing wall, about six and a half feet high, had shards of glass embedded along the top. They stuck out like thorns and cast glinting shadows of refracted light— a jagged rainbow like spattered hope. She bent over the custodian's shoulder and read the paper along with him. It was turned to the sports page; large red letters spelled FATE DECREES DEFEAT: ARIS LOSES ON PENALTY KICK.

"When we Greeks win, it's us; when we lose, it's fate," the custodian muttered to himself in disgust. He tossed the paper aside and looked up.

"New student?" he said.

There was no real curiosity in his eyes. He stared at her kindly enough, although totally unaffected by her presence, seeming merely to be taking in her stature and size. She was shaken. Grownups normally liked her.

"Ground floor. At the staircase, take a left, then a right, then a left again," he said. "You can't miss it—there's a plaque on the door."

Anna started walking back toward the building, but after a few steps, she turned around.

"Why the broken glass on top of the fence?" she asked.

"To keep boys from looking in."

"Looking at what?"

"You pretty girls."

He chuckled.

Anna did not see the joke. Why would boys want to climb

the fence and look in when they could look at girls all they wanted to on the streets?

"What kept you so long?" Aimilia asked when Anna returned.

"I took a stroll," Anna told her. "Satisfied?"

She walked on ahead fast. When she spotted the door with the plaque, she pointed.

"There it is!"

"I can see," Aimilia said. She pushed Anna out of the way, knocked on the door, and tried the knob. It was locked.

"No organization, no punctuality anywhere in this country," she said. "And we think we can get ahead!"

Anna read the name on the plaque: ARISTIDES ATHANASIADES, PRINCIPAL.

"In Alexandria, in my school, the principal and all the teachers were women," Aimilia said, watching her. "That's how it should be in a girls' school. You have to have models of the same sex."

Models? Anna thought. For what? She hated her women teachers—her men teachers, too, for that matter. They were cut-and-dried, passing on knowledge as though it were the law: "Two plus two equals four. There is one God. The capital of Italy is Rome." No one ever tried to explain why. Anna wanted to know why. It was hard to believe there had been a time, not so far back, when she had taken the world for granted, and had questioned only the sense, not the right and wrong, of things.

Heavy footsteps sounded down the hall. In a few moments, a tall middle-aged man with an unkempt, haphazardly fussy appearance approached. He had on a starched shirt, a rumpled suit, a tie, shoes with a spit shine. His hair was slicked back neatly, thinning but still dark. He walked self-absorbed and did not turn his eyes to them until he had put his key in the door.

"You may come in," he said.

He did not introduce himself, nor look at them directly as he beckoned them to sit down.

"Name?" he said, opening the ledger.

"Anna Karystinou."

He wrote it down, then reached out his hand.

"Papers."

Anna's elementary school diploma had the highest grade, and her entrance-exam certificate showed she had placed first in the region. Athanasiades looked at the marks, then up. A flicker of light passed through his eyes, but he did not smile.

"Anna Karystinou," he said finally, "I'm glad to have you in my school."

He got up from his desk and shook Anna's hand.

His fingers gripped hard, but the flesh on his palm lay inert to the pressure of her hand.

"Congratulations!" he said.

His approbation felt like censure, as if she were nothing in her own right but should fall and rise on his esteem.

"Say thank you," Aimilia said.

Anna looked down.

"Thank me?" Athanasiades said. "No, she does not need to thank me."

He stared at Aimilia with pressed civility.

"It's rare a girl places first," he said. "She's a special child—most special."

"She has quick perception but doesn't study hard enough," Aimilia said. "She has no discipline, no concentration. She doesn't do her homework."

"I very much doubt that."

Anna cowered. Aimilia had it right. The excellent marks and placing first on the exams were due to books she had read on her own—in the last year alone, *The Children's Encyclopedia*, in five volumes; three different histories of ancient Greece; *The World's Greatest Men, Gods and Heroes, The History of Christianity, The Lives of the Saints, Byzantium and the Crusades.* . . .

"I'm afraid she'll be like the hare of the fable, who was defeated by the turtle," Aimilia persisted.

Athanasiades shook his head. "Madam, if I were you, I'd be proud," he said. "Now, good day."

He turned to Anna, smiling with a proprietary air that made his slight to Aimilia all the more emphatic.

When they were outside the office, Aimilia bent back and looked down to make sure that the seams on her stockings were straight.

"You made a good impression. Don't undo it," she said to Anna as they began to walk away. "It would be most embarrassing if you failed this year."

"I've never failed."

"Elementary school is kid's stuff," Aimilia said. "*Now* we shall see."

They walked down the long, empty corridors in silence. As they were coming out onto the landing, an attractive girl walked through the gate, followed by a woman who resembled her. The woman fidgeted, brushing her hair away from her face, straightening her dress, twisting her rings in place. The girl walked with an impatient, clipped gait.

Anna felt a shiver run through her. It was the girl who had jumped over Saint John's fire first, the girl who had said to her, "Not one of the heathen?" She remembered her jumping, her legs wide open, her ponytail bouncing, and Anna suddenly felt as hot as she had that day. As then, a lulling quiver of heat as though from a fire within warmed her body and forced her to stand still.

The girl walked on up the steps. As she passed, her eyes sparked with recognition and she smiled, her lips parting with a slight tremor of delight, then setting firmly into a smirk.

"Sexy girl," Aimilia said. "A real looker, and she knows it. Reminds me of myself when I was that age."

"She dyes her hair."

"I know what you mean—the dark eyebrows—but I don't think so," Aimilia said. "The hair on her legs was light. A touch of peroxide maybe."

The girl's hair had a coarse shine. She wore it loose today. It fell around her face in frizzed, tangled clumps—bright, brittle, and wild, like sun-soaked autumn-dry thistle. Anna imagined putting her fingers in it softly, gently, clasping it at the roots—tugging at it till the girl screamed.

MONDAY MORNING, the first day of school, the sun shone hazy in a light blue sky, and the air was misty, languid with the lingering heat of the night before. It was unseasonably warm. Leaves and grass were still soft with sap, just beginning to turn. Fall always felt like the beginning of a new year. Sparse pale green tendrils pushing out of the frozen ground, scaly knobs like rupturing blisters on tree limbs— spring, at first, looked like blight. But, like sunset mirroring sunrise, in the splendor of autumn, there was a deepening calm, the promise of glorious new life to come. Everything was still in full leaf, a rich orange hue with splashes of brown and yellow. But even when everything withered and stood barren and forlorn, Anna loved fall. Its beauty became all the more forcible—like sadness that won't bend to pain.

She walked to school wary and expectant. She knew that her life was about to change once and for all. The street swarmed with girls, their uniforms like a black sea, white collars scalloping like foam on the crest of waves. When she passed the gate, the yard was so full she had to push her way through. No one seemed to notice her. She moved to the edge of the crowd and stood with her back against the fence wall.

The school uniforms made it hard to form a distinct

impression of any girl who caught her eye. After a while, she gave up. She did not see the girl with the wild hair approach. They were less than a yard apart when she became aware of her, and it gave her a start. She blushed, practically jumped.

"I'm Veronica Koroneou," the girl said. "You can call me Vera."

Her uniform was in a shirtwaist style, with a slinky gored skirt, straight sleeves, and a tailored collar. Anna blushed deeper. Her own uniform had pleats in front and buttons in back, full sleeves, and a round collar like a child's smock.

"Anna Karystinou," she said after a moment.

"We are going to be in the same class," Vera said. "The principal told me. 'The girl who was just here, before you,' he said, 'will be your classmate. She's special.' " She mimicked Athanasiades' voice, repeated, "Special!" and laughed. "At first, I thought he meant retarded. You looked like an idiot, you know—gawking, walking like you had lead in your joints." She moved away a few steps, then walked back, swaying rigidly from side to side, head thrust forward, eyes bulging. "The principal showed me your grades. He told me you placed first in the exam. Are you a genius?"

Anna thought her mind was bound by the rules of reason, like a common mind. She kept silent.

"I was first in *my* school, if you want to know. Give me a three-digit number and a two-digit one—any numbers you choose."

"Eight seventy-two and twenty-three."

"Multiplied, that makes . . . twenty thousand fifty-six."

Anna was amazed but tried not to show it.

"Who cuts your hair—the *barber*?" Vera said. "It looks like a boy's."

"If you want to know, Antoine cuts my hair."

They stared at each other's eyes silently a moment.

"What does your father do?" Vera asked.

"He's an army officer."

"Mine is a doctor." She bent over and whispered in Anna's ear, "He's a . . . gynecologist!"

Anna stepped back.

"Did he deliver you?"

"Just my last pregnancy."

"You know what I mean."

Again, they were silent, and again, it was Vera who spoke first.

"I have three brothers," she said.

"I have a younger sister."

"I'm a true-blooded Thessalonikian. You?"

"We have a house in Athens, but we've lived all over. My father is from Athens, and my mother comes from Egypt."

"Your mother is *Egyptian*!"

"No, Greek, of course! True-blooded Alexandrian."

"What is she, a descendant of Ptolemy?"

"Her parents and her grandparents were born there. Alexandria has a Greek community more cosmopolitan, more civilized, more affluent than any city in Greece proper."

"Says who?"

"Says I."

"Says *you*!"

They stared into each other's eyes, glowering, but in a moment broke into laughter.

"You know what this means—laughing together at the same time?" Vera said. "That we'll be friends—best friends. Want to bet?"

"I'm not betting we won't. We can't both bet we will."

"Yes, we can."

"Against whom?"

"Against fate. Shake on it?"

Vera had already reached out her hand; it would be an insult not to take it. Anna took her hand, cementing their pledge of friendship, but she felt tricked into it and it made her mad. She wasn't sure she liked Vera that much. She was smug and pretty—too pretty to trust. Anna tried to think of something to say to gain back ground, but there was a deafening screeching sound, then a garbled booming voice coming through the loudspeaker.

"New students, to the left of the yard! New students, to the left of the yard! Last names starting with *A* to *G* make up Section One. Last names starting with *H* to *L* make up Section Two. *M* to *R*, Section Three. *S* to *Z*, Section Four. Go to your sections and line up by height. Repeat! Go to your sections and line up by height."

There was sudden chaos—new girls stepping to the front, old ones stepping to the back.

Vera took hold of Anna's hand.

"*K*'s coming through!" she said, pulling Anna along. "*K*'s coming through!"

Girls were turning around to stare at them, and Anna was embarrassed. Vera did not seem to care. When they got to their section, she slumped so she and Anna would look the same height.

"I hope you grow taller soon, Karystinou, and catch up, or I'll get a humpback," she said.

Under the supervision of a teacher, the girls were already lining up, tallest first. When the line was complete, they were told to divide into ranks of four and form a column.

"All classes! All classes now!" the loudspeaker blared

again. "Line up in formations! . . . ATTEN-TTTION!!! At ease! We'll now say the Lord's Prayer."

Vera closed her eyes and mouthed the words to the Lord's Prayer soundlessly, aping pious devotion. When it came to the amen, she bellowed, "Ah me!" sighing.

She walked up closer to Anna and bumped hips. "Are you ready for the scholarly life?" she said.

Anna tensed up and walked on ahead, fast.

TWO OF THE classroom walls were covered with color engravings of heroes from the Greek Revolution, a third had continuous windows, and on the fourth, behind the teacher's podium, hung an icon of Christ on the cross and, directly below it, two photographs—of King Pavlos and Queen Frederiki. Bare lightbulbs on twisted cords hung equidistant along the middle of the ceiling. On either side of the podium were a blackboard and a map of Greece on easels.

The desks were lined up in two rows. The girls, sixty in all, sat four to a desk, their backs straight, forearms on the desktops, hands clasped, fingers entwined, totally still. It is all just like elementary school, Anna thought with dismay. Only the color of the uniforms had changed, from blue to black.

The teacher, standing, called the roll, closed her attendance book, and went down the aisle, correcting the girls' postures. She had on a gray flannel suit with a straight skirt, a blue fluted handkerchief in the breast pocket, no pin on the lapel, no scarf. Her shirt was white, stiff with starch. Her hair was pulled tight off her face and twisted in a bun.

"My name is Soteria Prokopiou and I'll be your philologist," she said after she had sat back down at her desk. "I'll be teaching you modern Greek, ancient Greek, Latin, and

history. I'm the teacher who'll be with you the greatest number of hours each day, so we'd better get along. If you need
to speak, raise your hand. I want no talking; I want no gig-
gling; I want no fidgeting in this class.

"Understood?"

"Yes, Miss Prokopiou."

She waved her hand, back side outward so they could see
her wedding band.

"Yes, *Mrs.* Prokopiou."

"Any questions?"

There were none.

"Good. I'm now going to give you the schedule for your
classes. I'll write it out so you can copy it."

She wrote the schedule on the blackboard, then sat at her
desk again.

"As you can see, today we start with modern Greek.
I'm going to read to you a story from your *Reader* entitled
'Alexander the Great and the Mermaid.' Open to page
twenty-three."

Anna left her *Reader* shut. If they had had to read "Alexander the Great and the Mermaid" in elementary school
once, they had had to read it a thousand times. They might
as well be Danaus's daughters, condemned to fill their sieves
with water—having to hear the story over and over. Blah,
blah, blah: A mermaid raised herself out of the waves each
time she saw a ship, seized its prow with her hands, and
asked, "Is Alexander the Great still alive?" If the seamen said
no, she sank their ship. If they said, "He lives and reigns and
the universe he claims," she let them go in peace. . . .

She glanced at Vera from the corner of her eye, and Vera
sneered and sighed. They were sitting side by side, Vera at
the outer edge of the desk, having claimed the seat as though

by peremptory right, Anna inside, next to a girl with a sickly pallor to her skin and nails bitten down to the quick. Turning and looking at her, Anna saw that she was holding her *Reader* up in her hands, head bowed, lips pursed, righteous and stern, like a deacon poring over his missal.

"'There was a legend about the Greek sea that had persisted to my day,'" Prokopiou read in a singsong declamatory voice. "'I say "legend." The seamen I met with in my youth, however, swore by its truth. What I'm about to relate to you is not one story. It's myriad stories told in myriad voices—it's the undying cry of hope in the hearts of all Greeks, the undying dream of glory. . . .'"

"Oh, mellifluous, brilliant prose!" Vera whispered.

"My very sentiments," Anna said. But her heart was not in the scorn she'd put in her voice. She was queasy with foreboding. Imagine, she thought—imagine if every class ends up being like this, what we already know, made more verbose. She listened attentively, thinking perhaps there was something different in this particular rendition of the tale— something more to it than the longer, fancier words.

"What does the story signify?" Prokopiou asked when she had finished reading. "You! You who are daydreaming!"

The girl she was addressing jerked up straight and looked at the teacher dumbfounded.

"What does the story signify?" Prokopiou repeated. "Anyone? What did Alexander the Great mean for Greece?"

There was no response.

"Am I teaching Greek women or am I teaching primates? What did Alexander the Great do?"

A girl sitting in a front desk raised her arm and said hesitantly, "He unified Greece and conquered the world."

"True. But what did he *accomplish* to be named Great?

Genghis Khan conquered the world, too, but we don't call him Great."

The girl had no answer to this.

"Which one of you is Anna Karystinou?"

Anna stood up.

"I'm told you are our best student this year. Tell us why—in your opinion—Alexander was a great man."

"He had bravery and pride and courage."

"So did Leonidas and the three hundred Spartans."

Anna lowered her head.

"When we stand up, Karystinou, we stand up straight, not hunched over like a beast of burden. What did Alexander the Great accomplish?"

Anna, not knowing the answer, blushed. She remained standing.

"What did Alexander do to be named Great?" Prokopiou asked again. "He changed the face of the earth—that's what he did. He civilized the East, spreading the Greek language and culture. He sowed the seed that, three centuries later, would allow Christianity to take hold."

Nonsense, Anna thought. There had been no missionary aspect to Alexander's character. The man had cried, it was said, when there were no more worlds to conquer. When one of his generals advised him to attack an encampment at night, surprising the enemy in their sleep, he answered, "I'm not a man who steals his victories." That was no mealymouthed world-civilizer talking! Alexander had conquered the world to test his mettle.

"That was not his intent," she said.

"History does not take intent into account," Prokopiou said. "You may sit down."

"Old sow!" Vera whispered. "You did great!" She tore a

page off her notebook and wrote, "Why did Alexander ask that his hands be left outside the winding-sheet when he died?"

Anna wrote underneath, "To show we all leave this world empty-handed—even great men."

"To show he wasn't playing with himself!!!"

"Ha! Ha!"

"Want to come home with me after school and eat with us? You'll get to meet my brothers."

"Tomorrow? I have to ask my parents."

"Tomorrow, then."

"Now we come to the textual analysis of the story. How many metaphors and how many similes do you find?" Prokopiou asked.

Vera wrote down, "Don't you want to DIE!!!"

"*Metaphorically* speaking!!!"

When the bell rang, they walked out arm in arm. As they were entering the yard, an upperclassman passed them, then turned to look at them, sizing them up with a mocking glance. Her hair was braided like a crown across the top of her head.

"Isn't she beautiful!" Anna whispered.

"She has cotton-candy brains. The personality of a boiled potato."

"How do you know?" Anna said, blushing.

"How do I know!" Vera said. "You're blushing! What is it with you? Your face is like an ambulance light."

Anna disengaged her arm. "Do you know anyone else here—from your grammar school?" she said after a while.

"I know a few girls."

"Weren't you friends with them?"

"My friends went on to private schools," Vera said. "My

mother wanted to send me to a private school, too, but my father believes public schools are better."

"Mine also. He says, 'Going to public school builds character.' "

"Right. Private school girls are snots. All my friends are snots. I don't speak to them anymore."

"I'm glad I'm your only friend," Anna said. "You're my only friend, too."

"You are my only friend *so far*," Vera said. But she paled as she said it.

Anna looked away.

"It's lucky we met," Vera said quickly. "I knew I was going to see you . . . again."

Anna still did not look at her. Then she turned, looked her straight in the face, and said, "And that's why you left—running?"

THE KORONEOUS' HOUSE was one story but stately, built in a neoclassic style, with marble pediments over the windows and front door. One entered through the waiting room of Dr. Koroneou's office, then went past sliding doors into a cavernous hall with a three-tier crystal chandelier. To the left and right, arched doorways led to the reception rooms—a library, a dining room, a double-size living room. The library was furnished sparsely and austerely, but the dining room and living room were crowded with massive ornate pieces—there was nowhere for the eye to rest without being caught in a tassel, curlicue, or trellis. The upholstery and curtains were of brocade, a uniform brown and gold. The side tables were draped with shawls trailing to the floor. Wallpaper depicting geese in flight over reed-filled marshes was interrupted at intervals by a confusion of oil portraits, watercolor landscapes, and lithographs of the ships that constituted the 1821 Greek revolutionary fleet. Silver- and leather-framed photographs, crystal ashtrays and vases, and porcelain and brass figurines gleamed gaudy and pristine, as in a store display.

Anna had followed Vera into the house and was standing next to her in the hall. Only the lowest tier of the chandelier was lit. The dim cascade of light fell onto the dark wood floor in a wide circle, diffusing into shadows at the outer edges. She could barely see the far wall.

"You want the grand tour now or later?" Vera said.

"Now."

"Follow me!"

They walked through the reception rooms.

"Do you spend much time here?" Anna asked.

"Birthday gatherings, funeral gatherings, holiday gatherings—which go with funeral gatherings. We lounge around in the basement normally."

"In the basement!"

"We burrow down like moles."

Anna tried to laugh.

"It's a *semi*basement," Vera said. "Relax. Practically a ground floor." She eased her school bag off her shoulders and let it drop onto the floor. "Mamakin!" she shouted, her voice making an echo. "I'm home!"

Mando Koroneou came out into the hall from the back of the house. She was wearing carpet slippers, a housedress, and a plastic apron. Her hair was fresh from the hairdresser, every curl lacquered into place, and there was makeup on her face. She must have gone out earlier, then come home and changed, Anna thought. She remembered her faintly from registration day. Her resemblance to Vera was extraordinary, though, unlike Vera, she was fat, which made her far, far lovelier in Anna's view. The puffy bulging of her breasts, the round mound of her belly, the plenitude of flesh stretching her dress like a second skin were beguiling, like a soft, trustful smile.

Taken off guard for liking her so immediately, so immensely, Anna offered her her hand with lowered eyes.

"I'm Anna."

"So you're Vera's new friend," Mando said. She laughed off Anna's proffered hand and gave her a hug. "My dove, my sweet girl," she said, squeezing her in her arms.

"Mamakin, let her go!" Vera yelled. "Really!"

Anna pulled back, blushing.

"If you don't watch out," Vera said to her, "she'll clobber you with kisses."

Mando shook her head, looking with forbearing tenderness at her daughter.

"Ah," she said. "I *have* to leave you. I have to go turn over my fish."

She hurried back to the kitchen.

"You want to go out to the yard?" Vera said.

Before Anna could answer, the sliding doors at the entrance to the hall drew open, and both girls turned around.

"Papakin," Vera said, standing as though frozen.

Anna was surprised. Dr. Koroneou seemed to be in his seventies. He had a craggy, severe face, totally white hair and eyebrows. There was a forbidding air about him. He was very tall, thin but broad-shouldered, and walked with a lax, slow gait—the solemn ease of a sovereign surveying his realm.

"Do I ask who you are, or will your esteemed friend remember her manners and introduce us?" he said to Anna as he approached.

"Anna Karystinou," Anna said, shaking his hand. His fingers were cold, bone-dry on her skin, his grip so tight, it hurt.

"You knew who she was," Vera said. "I told you last night she was having lunch with us."

" '*She!*' See what I mean?" Dr. Koroneou said, staring keenly into Anna's eyes. "No savoir faire, your friend." He turned to his daughter for the first time. "How is it I haven't gotten my kiss?"

Vera raised herself on tiptoes and kissed him on the cheek. He did not bend to her.

"Now then," he said. "In we go and eat. Anna, my dear, you'll have the rare privilege of sampling one of Mrs. Koroneou's charred specialties. I smell burned fish."

He went on ahead. Anna expected him to turn into the dining room, but he went on to the back of the house.

"What about our school bags?" she whispered.

"We'll leave them here. Mamakin will get them later," Vera said. "Come on!"

Anna's bag leaned against the wall. Vera's lay in the middle of the floor, where she'd dropped it. Anna started toward the back of the house, then turned around. She picked up her bag and put it next to Vera's. Now they both lay in the middle of the floor.

THE KORONEOUS had three sons. Christophoros was eighteen, in the last year of high school. He looked like his father but had a gentler expression. Though not as tall, he was more muscular. He had a passionate nature and was handsome, serious, and melancholy—attractive in the compelling and disquieting way of a young man still unsure of his manhood. Fotis and Nikitas were fourteen years old, identical twins. They resembled no one else in the family and seemed a separate entity from the rest. Their faces were plump and broad, with hair shorn close to the scalp, their bodies shapeless with the extra bulk adolescents sometimes put on before growing tall. They talked with aggressive assurance, completing or echoing each other's thoughts; when they were silent, an expression of alert, sly passivity settled in their eyes—so alike, so simultaneous, it was uncanny.

When Vera walked into the kitchen, her family was already seated. She took her place at the table without acknowledging anyone's presence. Anna, coming in a moment later, hesitated by the door.

"Christophoros, Fotis, Nikitas," Vera said, pointing.

Anna looked from brother to brother. Vera had told her Fotis and Nikitas were twins, but had not mentioned they were identical, and Anna couldn't help staring. Christophoros stood up as she approached, and he remained on his feet till she sat down, giving her cursory, if polite, glances. He seemed so unimpressed by her, his courtesy was abashing. He was the most attractive young man Anna had ever seen. It was not his face alone, but something about his tense, sad presence: something—she realized, amazed—about the muscles on his shoulders and arms. She had never found a man's body beautiful before. It made sense when someone's eyes or mouth were beautiful, for the beauty of the eyes and mouth was the beauty of the soul. But the body? Mere flesh? She could not fathom what that was. Liking him made her anxious.

"Come sit down," Vera said, rattling the empty chair next to hers.

Anna sat down and unfolded her napkin. It was paper, too small to lay on her lap. At her home, they took all meals, except for breakfast, in the dining room. There was always a linen tablecloth and matching napkins. Fork, knife, spoon, glass, and plates were set neatly in their proper place. Stephanos sat at the head of the table, Aimilia and Maritsa to his left, Anna to his right. Once the food was on the plates, no conversation was allowed. Here, the table was covered with oilcloth; plates, glasses, and silverware were everywhere. The table was round, with no apparent established order. The food—platters of fried mullets, steamed greens, and mashed potatoes—was being passed around every which way.

"Ve*ka*ra*ka*, dear*ka*, sis*ka*ter*ka*," said Fotis, heaping mashed potatoes onto his plate. "You've*ka* got*ka* sauce*ka* on*ka* your*ka* nose*ka*."

"That's*ka* not*ka* sauce*ka*," said Nikitas. "That's*ka* snot*ka*." He turned to Mando. "Moth*ka*er*ka*," he said to her, "your*ka* daugh*ka*ter*ka* is*ka* a snot*ka*nose*ka*."

He poured himself a glass of water and slurped it.

"Nikitas!" Mando reprimanded in a mild voice.

"The Japanese consider it good manners," Nikitas retorted. He pulled at the sides of his eyes and lisped, "We Japanese most well-brought-up people."

Fotis placed his hands under his chin, palm on palm, as if in prayer. "*Eeeh eeeh oh, eeeh eeeh oh,*" he sang through his nose.

"That's the Chinese, stupid," Vera said.

Dr. Koroneou made no attempt to scold or interfere. Anna looked at him, expecting at least a disapproving scowl, but he seemed indifferent. Without bothering to conceal his distaste for the food, he ate with sullen, methodical insistence, a pile of fish heads and backbones amassing neatly at the edge of his plate.

Christophoros, who apparently did not like mullet, had been served grilled lamb chops and was gnawing gingerly at a bone. Oblivious to Anna's presence, impervious to the clowning and commotion of the twins, he was wrapped in himself with an intensity Anna could feel.

She swallowed uncomfortably. The mullets had been, indeed, burned to a crisp. The twins stared at her relentlessly, and trying to smile while not amused was straining every fiber in her face.

Judging by Christophoros's age, Mrs. Koroneou must be around forty, she thought. She remembered what Stephanos said about women: As the Spartans kill crippled babies at birth, in an ideal society, women should be disposed of at forty.

He said, "Once women stop pleasing the eye or bearing children, they've outlived their use."

He said, "As the healthy recoil from the sick, so the male recoils from the ugly female."

He said, "A woman born ugly is a freak of nature; a woman who lets herself become fat and repulsive is an insult to manhood."

There was no graver offense than insulting manhood. It abutted sin. How could a woman who had given birth to three sons insult manhood?

Pleasing *whose* eye?

He wouldn't like Mando, even if it weren't for her age. Her body brought to mind sheaves of fresh-cut wheat. Dry summer heat. The acrid smell of laborers' sweat and mown sap.

Anna and her father just didn't have the same tastes. Among flowers, he liked calla lilies and tight petaled roses best, whereas she loved soft, humble flowers like sweet peas, anemones, cyclamens, poppies—flowers you could bury your face in. It did not do to cut them; they wilted in a vase. But rooted in the earth, their gentle hardiness broke the heart.

"There're those of us who talk in our sleep; there're those of us who walk in our sleep," Vera stage-whispered to the twins. "This here girl eats in her sleep."

She nudged Anna's arm. "Wake up!"

Startled, Anna jangled her fork loudly on her plate. Christophoros looked up, stared at her distractedly, then gradually smiled, with the amused kindness one directs at an awkward child. She blushed, and he looked away, the smile deepening on his face. He continued to eat.

There was silence. Mando pushed the mullet platter in Anna's direction.

"Some more?"

So as not to give offense, Anna took another mullet.

"One!" Mrs. Koroneou said. "One is none."

She pushed three more mullets onto Anna's plate. Anna ate them fast, gulping water after each bite.

"What did you do with the bones on your plate?" Vera asked.

"I ate them."

"You *ate* them! You ate the backbones?"

"They were small."

"People! People!" Vera shouted, taking Anna's plate from her and showing it off. "Anna ate all the bones!"

"Who is she?" Fotis asked Nikitas.

"She's Anna."

"Anna who?"

"Anna Phosphorus."

"What does Anna do?"

"She glows."

"Anna Phosphorus?"

"Anna Phosphorus!"

Anna kept her eyes down.

"Why does Anna Phosphorus glow?"

"Because she eats fish bones."

"Anna Phosphorus?"

"Nikitas! Fotis!" Mando said. "Enough!"

She started to clear the table.

"Mrs. Koroneou, it was a delicious meal," Anna said. "I'd like to—"

"Yes, yes, yes—great food! Mamakin, Anna would like to thank you," Vera said. "Let's go!"

She pulled Anna up from her chair, yanking her arm.

"You aren't one of those people who needs to take a nap?" she asked when they were out the door.

Anna shook her head.

"Good. Me neither."

They went back into the front hall, and on to the waiting room, then to Dr. Koroneou's office. It was a small room with a Persian rug, a large desk, two leather armchairs, and a bookcase filled with gold-embossed leather-bound books in meticulous order. Engravings of the harbor and different views of the city as it had looked a century ago hung on the walls.

Anna expected they would sit in the armchairs and talk, but Vera opened the door to the examining room and pushed her inside.

"I thought you'd like to see this," she said.

Here, the floor was bare—black hexagonal tiles—the walls white. In a glass case, there was a display of medical instruments in mutations of normal designs—curved scissors, rounded clamps, concave spatulas—deformed yet horrifyingly precise. There was no examining table. The only other things in the room were a sink, a metal shelf, and a reclining chair with metal extensions at the lower end. Anna surmised that the chair was constructed so as to accommodate cripples. The metal extensions would be where they rested their legs after taking the braces off.

"Your father delivers babies, you said?"

"Not anymore. He's a gynecologist only."

Anna wondered about the need for separate doctors for men and women. Girls went to the same doctors as boys.

"What do gynecologists do exactly?" she asked.

"They look up women's cunts."

"Why?"

"Why do other doctors look down your throat? You go to a gynecologist when you have a sore cunt. It's the same thing. You get infections and things."

Anna was stunned.

"They use *tongue depressors* to look in?"

Vera nodded. "When a man goes to a doctor," she said, "the doctor puts a finger in his asshole. It evens out."

"No man lets a doctor put a finger up his . . . *that*," Anna said vehemently. "No doctor would dare do it, either."

"Oh yeah?" Smirking, Vera went back out into her father's office.

"Now what?" Anna was annoyed.

"Want to see a book that will turn your hair on end?"

Anna shrugged.

"Hide under the desk, in case someone comes."

Anna crawled under.

"Wait! Stay there!" Vera said. "I'll get a flashlight."

When she came back, she handed Anna a big, heavy book.

"You turn the pages," she said, crawling under the desk. "I'll shine the light."

The book was filled with close-up photographs of male and female genitals—misshapen, covered with lesions, sores, and warts. Anna looked on with shame and fascination. When closed, women's genitals were no different from baby girls'—

a crack, like the soft corner of a smile. Opened up, they were horrifying—the parted thick fuzz of hair like gashed fur, the glistening crinkled dark folds of skin like the slashed underbelly of a slain beast. Men's genitals were repulsive but innocuous, like sleep-sluggish obese worms. But so big! On little boys, they were no bigger than their noses.

She was getting hot; she could feel her underarms drenched in sweat. They were cramped under the desk, touching shoulder to shoulder, hip to hip. She could hear her heart pounding, Vera's, too. It was making her tense, the sound of it, she couldn't breathe. When they'd looked at the last picture, she crawled out from under the desk, gasping for air.

Vera followed after her, flushed—red from head to foot.

They stood apart. Uncomfortable as she'd been under the desk, Anna wanted to be closer, to have their bodies touch again. She felt anxious suddenly, because they had looked at the pictures, hiding—on the sly. Vera seemed anxious, too. She wouldn't look Anna in the eye, kept shifting her weight from leg to leg as though she wanted to run out but was holding back.

"Let's go out in the yard," Vera said.

Anna followed her out of the room. After a few steps, she reached out to touch Vera's back.

Vera jumped. "I want you to meet Zephyr," she said quickly.

"Who's Zephyr?"

"My cat."

Her cat! Anna wanted them to embrace, to make the anxiety go away, and Vera wanted to show her some cat.

The yard was enclosed by a high stone wall. Tall, big-branched mulberry trees and lilac and pomegranate bushes rose randomly above knee-deep grass and weeds. In the center, under a canopy of grapevines and jasmine, was a moss-covered well that had a rusted, broken winch. The narrow pebble path that led to and around it gleamed in the shadows from the grass like a gray snake. It was humid and warm, the sun shone in a hazy blue sky, the air smelled of damp earth and mulch.

Vera skipped down the steps and ran through the garden, yelling, "Zeph-yyyr! Zeph-yyyyyr!"

Anna watched from the porch, holding on to the iron railing. Her hands felt moist and grainy, and a metallic taste was on her tongue. She opened her hands and looked, horrified, at her palms. They were covered with rust, caked and brown like dried blood.

When she next looked up, Vera was at the far end of the garden, turned toward the house. She was standing in a small clearing, next to a rock. The sun was on her face, and she had shaded her eyes with her hand. She gazed at Anna steadily, as if she wanted her to come near.

Anna stayed where she was, her arms stiff and slightly lifted so her soiled hands would not touch her clothes.

VERA'S ROOM was in bright pink. It had a white rug with a pink floral motif, pink lace curtains, a pink ruffled bedspread, pink ruffled pillows, pink lamp shades, a vanity with a pink organdy skirt, and a pink armoire that had glass doorknobs in the shape of open roses. Mounted on a pedestal in a corner was an oversize marquise doll with white pompadoured hair and a magenta dress. She was covered with cellophane that hung over her like a bell jar. The only plain wood furniture was the bookcase under one of the windows and a large oak desk.

Vera was sprawled across her bed with pillows propped behind her back, one arm bent over her forehead and the other listless at her side, palm up. All her room needed, she thought, was pink flies on the walls—flies that shat pink shit. She stared Anna in the eyes and smirked, showing her that she was the first to mock the room's decor. But Anna gave no sign she was about to speak. She had walked straight to the desk, had pulled out the chair, and had lowered herself stiffly onto it without a word. Now she was sitting with her legs open, her hands clasped to the edges of the seat on either side of her thighs, her back rigid against the backrest. The visit was not going the way Vera expected. She had been sure she'd have Anna eating out of her hand. But Anna was ignoring her, staring down at her shoes. They were brand-new, and there was a red swelling on the top of her feet, where shoe met skin.

"It's low-class to wear loafers without socks," Vera told her.

"I have low-class feet," Anna said.

Anna walked to the bookcase with a deliberately slow gait and looked through the shelves. "I have all her books, too," she said.

"Whose?"

"Penelope Delta's. She's the greatest."

Vera had not read Delta since she was eleven. Even then, she had known her books were idealistic, sentimental pulp. "She's pretty good when you're a little kid," she said.

She got up from the bed and joined Anna.

" 'Pretty good'?" Anna said. "She's the greatest. Hands down, no contest, absolutely the greatest. Did you know she killed herself when the Germans overran Greece?"

"She had been sick."

"She had not. It was out of patriotism. You can tell how patriotic she was from her books. . . . Can you imagine—can you *imagine*—killing yourself because your country has been defeated!"

"I'm telling you, she was sick."

"What did she have, if you know so much?"

"I don't know what, precisely."

"You shouldn't talk then."

Anna walked back to Vera's desk, took her books out of her school bag, and slammed them down.

"That's my desk," Vera yelled. "No one bangs on it—you hear! Penelope Delta wrote shit."

"Obviously, you know nothing about literature."

"Penelope Delta wrote books for children. If you think that's literature, you're a blockhead."

Anna made no reply. She opened up her history book and pretended to study.

Vera got out her own history book. "We should read aloud to each other," she said. "We should take turns."

"I'll start."

"I'll start. It's my house."

Vera started reading. She could not see Anna, with her eyes on the page, but she could feel her presence all the more strongly—all the more insufferably. She was pigheaded. She was ignorant. She was dense. Moment to moment, there was no guessing what she might do or say next. She had a totally transparent face, yet the better you saw through her, the more you ended up being thrown for a loop. It was like skating blithely along and then suddenly skidding to a stop over thin ice. You could see through it all right.

"Your turn," she said when she came to the end of the page. She was too angry to concentrate.

Anna picked up where Vera had left off, softly moving her lips, the rest of her face remaining still. Her back, her neck, and her head were straight, yet they had a supple grace. Once she started reading, she completely relaxed.

Vera kept fidgeting. She tried to pay attention, but the words burst upon her ears like waves breaking over rocks. She stared at Anna's eyebrows with envy. They sloped down to the corners of her eyes, looked like a swallow's wings before flight. Her own made narrower curves, and they needed constant plucking or they'd grow into bushy cones.

"Are you listening to what I'm reading?" Anna said.

She closed the book and slumped, letting her right leg slide, bending her head to the side. Her body draped languidly over the hard edges of the chair; her skirt rode up her thighs, revealing a funnel of deepening shadow, a gleam of soft white skin.

My eyes are a nicer color, Vera thought. I have fuller lips . . . dimples when I smile.

"Were *you* listening to what you were reading?" she said.

"No."

They burst into raucous, tense laughter.

"It means—" Vera said, trying to stop laughing. "It means—"

"It means we are friends." Anna sneered, then turned bright red almost immediately.

She looked practically apoplectic. Vera reeled back and waited anxiously for the moment to pass.

"Has anyone ever told you you have a twitch?" Vera said.

"In your left eye. Not now," she added quickly. "But you do . . . sometimes."

She took some pumpkin seeds out of the desk drawer, gave Anna a handful, and sat on top of the desk. After a while, Anna climbed up and sat next to her.

Vera swung her legs back and forth to keep from jumping off. Anna had sat down too close; Vera could feel her breathing.

"Let's see who can spit out the hulls the farthest," she said.

Anna tried to spit out a hull, puckering her lips.

"Not like that! You have to use your tongue. Spit! *Spit!* Like this." Vera flicked her tongue in and out of her mouth. She propelled a hull toward the wall. "See?"

Anna tried to imitate her, without success. "It's just as well," she said. "I like eating the hulls."

"You shouldn't. Nikitas liked eating them, too, and his appendix burst last year."

Anna raised her skirt, pulled down her underpants, and pointed to the right side of her stomach. "I've had my appendix out," she said.

Vera leaned over to see the scar. It lay beneath thick pubic hair and was barely visible. Her own pubic hair was scraggly, nothing but wispy blond strands, but she had a scar that outdid Anna's by far. She jumped off the desk, flipped up her skirt, and bent over, lowering her pants.

"I had a boil that had to be lanced," she said.

"It must have hurt like hell."

"Does it look awful?"

"Not really awful," Anna said hesitantly. "Fortunately, it's where no one can see it."

"Except—you know—"

Anna's face went blank; then she blushed.

"You *don't* know," Vera said.

"I do so," Anna protested. "The man lies on top of the woman, and they're both stark naked. I don't know why everyone gets that mean, smutty look in their eye when they talk about it—that's what I don't know." She crossed her legs tight at the knees and clenched her fists. "It just galls me," she said. "You can't be in a new crowd for an instant without some boy baiting you to see if you 'know.' Next time I shake someone's hand, I'm going to say, 'I'm Anna Karystinou and, yes, I do know about sex.' "

Vera sniggered. "When a man fucks a woman," she said, "his you-know-what—"

Anna cut her off. "Can we change the subject?" she said.

She dragged the desk chair to the center of the room and sat down, letting her legs sprawl. She was directly in the passage to the balcony. The doors were open, the drawn curtains bellowed softly in the warm afternoon breeze, and the dappled light that passed through trembled about the chair.

Vera looked away.

"You want to see my actor photos?" she said after a moment.

"Oh, all right," Anna said.

Vera took her actor photos from the bottom bureau drawer, walked back, and thrust them into Anna's hand. She couldn't believe this was happening. Anna had appropriated her chair, she was sitting right in the center of her room, and she, Vera, had to flutter about at the edges, carrying and fetching.

"Who's this?" Anna said.

"James Dean."

"I don't know him."

"You've never seen *Rebel Without a Cause?* You've never seen *East of Eden?*"

Anna shook her head.

Vera showed her all her James Dean photos.

"He pouts," Anna said.

" 'Pouts'? That's all you can say—he *pouts?*" She passed her the Montgomery Clifts. "I bet you don't know him, either."

"I like the first one better," Anna said. "He has more spunk, at least."

" 'At least,' " Vera said, mimicking Anna's voice and rolling her eyes. "If you saw James Dean in a film, you'd fall for him, I guarantee it."

Anna looked through the James Dean photos again but did not say anything.

"Which movie star is your favorite?" Vera asked her.

"Dirk Bogarde."

"I've never heard of him. You're making him up—you're blushing."

"I'm not! He's British." She had turned completely red. "He was in this one film I saw, where he played a double role," she said. "He was a nobleman, who was good, and another man, who was evil."

"Him!" Vera said. "*Libel?* You don't mean *Libel!* That was pure melodramatic muck."

"I concede it was sentimental."

"Sappy," Vera said. "It was *sappy*. And that Bogarde man looked like a fop, when he didn't look plain nasty. You should have your head examined."

"He was playing a role."

"All too well," Vera said. She walked out to the balcony.

It was siesta time and the street was empty, the shutters of the houses closed. A sparrow hopped from branch to branch to the top of the tree across the way and started twittering. She wanted to cry. She did not know why.

Anna had followed her out and was leaning against the railing, a few steps away.

"How can you like someone who's evil?" Vera asked.

"Evil people are proud."

"Pride is a sin."

"It is not. Pride is knowing who you are and being true to it," Anna said. "I like *you* because you're proud."

Vera started to cry silently, tears flooding over. She did not know what she was feeling—angry . . . happy . . . sad. The tears kept coming, and it was impossible to stop them.

Anna stepped closer and touched her on the shoulder.

Vera tried not to move away. First just in the part that Anna pressed gently with her hand, then through her entire arm, then through her whole body, it was as if there were no clothes, skin, flesh, bone—nothing but a feeling of love. In emptiness it stirred—helpless, alone.

IT WAS NIGHT when Anna left Vera's house. Rather than taking the well-lit avenue that ran along the harbor, she used the back way, a shortcut. There was no traffic or people on the street. The light from windows—two or three in each house, and scattered far apart—was diffused in the darkness, glistening on the leaves of trees like a shadow. Her footsteps reverberated and echoed, as though the darkness were impenetrable just beyond. She tried to will away the fear, but it was like trying to sleep while in the grip of a nightmare.

As she walked on, the darkness seemed to deepen. Fog

was drifting in from the sea, moving close to the ground in patches like flat clouds. She could no longer see the facades of the houses lining the street. They became gray shadows—ghosts of houses. There was barely a wind, but she could hear a loose shutter rattling and the chains of a swing creaking slowly and steadily, as when one sways without lifting one's feet. She was terrified. The fear had lodged between her shoulder blades, and she could feel it throb, pounding in the certainty that something stealthy and vile was biding its time to take her from behind. It was unlike any fear she'd had before. She did not know exactly what it was she feared.

It seemed as though she did not know anything about the world, suddenly—as though she were walking the earth alone and had no place to go.

She thought of Vera, cozy in her rich house. She lived in a city she could call her own; she would keep living here after Anna was gone in a year, and give her no further thought.

Every time she moved to a new place, she told herself not to make new friends, not to let herself care, and here she was, down the same old road. She could pretend not to care—she could make it not show—but in the end the hurt would be all the worse. It always was.

She didn't want to go home. Frightened as she was, she wished she could keep walking—walk and never have to stop.

When she reached the street she lived on, she rounded the corner and stood still. In the bleary light, the lantern by the churchyard glowed like a misty amber moon. Her house receded from the street, as though afloat in the fog. Only one window was lit. Aimilia was standing behind it, looking out—her silhouette, dark and immobile, like the pupil of a single, horrifying eye.

Eleven Days in December

IT WAS MIDDAY FRIDAY, the second week in December. The vases in the living room were filled with chrysanthemums. They were the last of the season, the last from the garden, with lush, plentiful leaves and stunted blossoms. Stephanos wondered if they were called "flowers of mourning" because they lasted in water a long time. They were beginning to give off a fetid scent, though the shaggy petals still had an unfading waxy sheen, curling sprightfully at the edges.

He had come home a short time ago, and he was still in uniform, with his military cap on, sitting on the edge of the armchair seat, elbows on thighs, his right hand between his knees, a cigarette burned to a stub in his fingers. He put it out and reached for a new one. The cigarette pack lay next to Aimilia's abandoned solitaire game, crooked, sloppy columns of cards that looked as if they had been slapped in place. He guessed the game would have come out. She did not play to the end if she could tell it was a win, folding with the same futility as when she lost.

He blew out smoke and watched it drift in the sunlight like dispersing fog. Why play at all? he thought, picking up the paper he'd brought home. The lead story was on the last murder, the ninth so far. The only new information was that forensic evidence had definitively determined it was the work of a serial killer. Everyone, including police in their official statements, was now referring to him as "the Dragon." Mythologizing was a way of denying the horror of existence. He'd lost the capacity for it. You've been through a war, you leave mythmaking to poets and priests. The civil war had purged him of any belief that human nature has moral bounds. He'd seen officers maim and violate captured men, strangling them with bare hands, beating them to death. Both sides did it. To say that not everyone committed such acts was not to say everyone was not guilty. Whoever bore witness also bore complicity. He'd refrained—not because there was more good in him, he thought, merely more dignity. People considered murder, not sanctioned by a cause, aberrant. But it was survival's rule.

He had killed, and there was no getting around it. It was not a matter of remorse; remorse begged a lie, bolstering self-esteem. It was a matter of owning up to the deed— suffering the knowledge.

"Come here, will you?" Aimilia called out to him from the kitchen.

He folded the paper and got up.

"Did you hear me?" she called out again. "Are you there?"

Without answering, he walked to the kitchen. She did not turn to look at him, but remained with her back to him, head bent, humming to herself. She was mixing chopped meat with onions and bread crumbs in a bowl.

"What do you want?"

"Can you get me the saltshaker? I don't want to get grease on it from my hands."

He searched the spice shelf but could not find the saltshaker.

"Look on the dining room table," she said.

He went into the dining room, brought back the salt-shaker, and poured some salt on her palm.

She asked for oregano, cumin, pepper—one thing at a time, so he had to go back and forth.

"If you used your mind to *think*, you'd put the herbs and spices in the mixing bowl before you put in the meat—before you got grease on your hands."

"You don't put them in before the meat," she said. "Any more advice?"

Scattered, smeared, and speckled all over the table were eggshells, milk, onion peel, bread crumbs, mint stems, and grease, but the front of her dress was spotless. She managed to remain untouched in the mess she created—in everything, always. Now she sang to herself, ignoring him.

> *Oh Eleni*
> *I know I'm no good*
> *But love you all the same*
> *Believe your heart*
> *Believe your eyes, Eleni*
> *What did they tell you against me*
> *What makes you cry*
> *When I pass by*
> *I know I'm no good*
> *but love you all the same*

He went back to the living room and turned on the radio to shut out her voice.

It was the news: ". . . Police would not disclose the nature of the latest forensic evidence but confirmed it indicates—"

He turned it off.

"What was that?" she shouted from the kitchen.

He did not answer her.

"I spoke to you!"

She came into the living room and stood opposite him, two feet away from his chair.

"What was that about the murder?"

She saw the paper on the coffee table, picked it up, and started to read, first standing up, then sitting on the sofa.

"Did you read this?"

A strand of hair had fallen over her eyes and she tossed it back with her hand, palm outward—a feckless gesture, like a child's. Her face was tense with concentration. She read the article, then repeated the information to him. Whatever she read, whatever she did, whatever she saw, she had to recount. Reality took no hold in her mind unless she put it in spoken words.

"Why are you staring at me like that?" she asked.

He looked away, at the window. The branch of the syca-more tree shivered in the wind. It was leafless, still wet from the recent rain, and its bark gleamed in the sun like oiled skin.

"Shouldn't the children be home already?" he said.

"Maritsa is eating upstairs. Anna—" They heard the front door open. "Speak of the devil."

There was the sound of footsteps, then Anna's voice say-ing, "This way."

"Christ, I forgot she was bringing her friend," Aimilia said, rushing back to the kitchen.

Stephanos hesitated, then got up from his chair. He had

not met Anna's new friend and had heard very little about her. He expected to see a plain, demure girl—the studious type. He was so taken aback, he knew the surprise and pleasure had shown on his face. The girl blushed but met his eyes and held him in her gaze without a smile. She walked up to him with a subtle sway at the hips, more taunting than seductive. This one went for the kill.

Anna had not moved from the doorway. "My friend Vera," she said, looking hard at his face.

He extended his hand and Vera shook it, shy suddenly—nervous.

"Can we go now?" Anna said.

She walked over and put her arm around Vera's shoulders. "Can we go now?" she said again.

They walked away.

Stephanos stared at Vera's retreating back. She stumbled, feeling him, but righted herself without turning to look back. Unexpectedly, it was Anna who turned her head over her shoulder. She stared at him, then turned quickly away, but not before he could see the hatred in her eyes.

He remembered the day of her baptism, walking from house to church, holding her in his arms. The village they were in had been ransacked and laid to ruin during the war. What houses remained stood among crumbled walls and burned tree stumps. The villagers had not yet risen from their midday sleep, and the street was silent and empty, the radiance of the soft afternoon sun holding the air still. She was unaccustomed to being carried and lay stiff in his arms. From the day she was born, he had forbidden Aimilia to cuddle her, making her rest her on a pillow while she nursed. It should teach her that you get out of life only what you take yourself. If he was present, he took the nipple out of her mouth while she fed to make her fight and reach for it. But on that day, feeling her unresponsive to his touch, her small weight pressing rigidly against his chest and arms, he thought he'd cry for the tenderness he had made himself suppress. Like the weeds growing in the ruins around him, her small life was pushing through the cracks in his heart, filling and rending them apart. Will she, he had thought, one day understand? Will she know that to hold back, when one must, is love? He could never have imagined then that his love would breed hate.

BEFORE THEY SAT down to lunch, Anna warned Vera that they would not be allowed to talk. "It's a rule in our house," she explained. "When we eat, we eat; when we speak, we speak." Vera forbore comment. But then Anna added, "There won't be any water on the table. Drinking water with a meal is forbidden."

"When you eat, you eat; when you drink water, you drink water. I understand."

"Seriously," Anna persisted. "Water dilutes the stomach fluids."

"That stands against custom all over the world. Even animals drink water with their food."

"*After* they eat," Anna said. "We do, too, after—or before. You can drink up to half an hour before. Perhaps you should have a glass of water right now."

"No thanks."

Vera had made it through the meal with her eyes fastened on her plate. The Karystinous not only did not talk but made no noise whatsoever while they ate. Her knife and fork were the only ones that clanged—like a leper's bell warning off the hale.

Now Anna and she were sitting out on the kitchen porch, thankfully alone. It was no wonder she had not asked Vera to the house before. Not that she actually seemed embarrassed to have such strange parents: She was reading aloud to Vera from the paper, nonchalant and in perfect repose, her feet on the porch railing and her back curved like a scythe.

"What I don't understand is how the paper can say there's been no evidence of violence when the victims have been murdered."

"That's *violation*, blockhead," Vera told her. She put her feet up on the railing, too. "That means sex."

Anna blushed.

"How would you kill someone if you wanted to kill someone?" Vera asked her.

"I'd bash their head against the wall."

"You're just saying that because of what you've read about the Dragon."

"I *am* not. He uses a rock. I wouldn't use a rock. I would take them by the hair and *bang bang bang* against the wall, till their skull cracked. Or maybe against the floor, if I could get them down. How would you do it?"

"I would stab them with a knife through the heart."

"When I'm angry at someone, it's their brains I want to squash," Anna said.

"I wasn't asking about killing someone because you're angry at them. I was asking about killing someone because you hate them."

"I've never thought about that. I haven't hated anyone that much, I don't think. Have you?"

"Uh-huh."

They had been talking without looking at each other, gazing at the garden. Anna turned from the waist and looked at Vera intently. "Who?"

"This girl I knew in sixth grade," Vera said. "Jasmine."

"Why did you hate her?"

"I hated her name for one. *Jas-mine* . . ."

"You wanted to knife her for her name?"

"She had adenoids," Vera said. "She was fat. She wore her skirts down to her calves. She just rubbed me the wrong way."

"Deserved to die!"

"No, but I'm serious. I did wish her dead. *Violated*—that's your new word for today, Karystinou—and murdered."

They stared in silence out at the garden. A flower bed had been recently dug up and filled with manure, and the smell wafted through the air—now faint, now strong.

"So, whom else have you wanted to knife?" Anna said.

"Whose head have you wanted to bash?"

"I asked you."

"I started the discussion."

"Everybody's I know, when I'm angry," Anna said.

"Mine, too?"

"Not yet."

Vera turned her head and looked at her, but Anna avoided her eyes.

"Let's go to my room. I'm getting cold," she said.

Vera had had a forbidding glimpse of Anna's room when they'd gone in to leave their bags. It had looked like a prison or a monk's cell. On second glance, it seemed less dismal, but certainly austere. There was a cot made up with military blankets, a metal night table, a small desk with a wooden chair, a low bookcase under one of the windows, and an armoire with a brown curtain instead of a door. The only beautiful thing in the room was a gold-embossed leather-bound book that lay on the night table. She picked it up. It was a copy of an old edition of Marcus Aurelius's *Meditations*. The inscription on the flyleaf read: "To my only son. We are born animals; we learn to be men."

"My father gave it to me for my last birthday," Anna told her.

" 'To my only son'?"

"My grandfather wrote that," Anna explained. "My father's father. He gave it to my father on *his* thirteenth birthday. I've been reading it every night before going to sleep."

Vera glanced at the beginning: "1. Courtesy and serenity of temper I first learnt to know from my grandfather Verus. 2. Manliness without ostentation I learnt from what I have heard and remember of my father. 3. My mother set me an example of piety and generosity. . . ." It went on like the begats in Genesis, naming fifteen more people who had inspired him to virtue. There were twelve books in all. She flipped through the pages. Book Two concluded: "And last and chief, wait with good grace for death, as no more than a simple dissolving of the elements each living thing is composed of. If those elements themselves take no harm from their ceaseless forming and re-forming, why look with mistrust upon the change and dissolution of the whole? It is but Nature's way; in the ways of Nature there is no evil to be found."

Wait with good grace for death! Vera thought.

"It's hard going," Anna said.

"I'll say!"

Anna looked over Vera's shoulder at the passage Vera had

just read to herself. "The elements of which each living thing is composed comprise the body, not the soul," she said. "There *is* evil in the ways of nature. There is evil in man—in *his* nature."

"Absolutely there is," Vera said. "I'd like to know how Marcus Aurelius would explain away the Dragon."

"He'd say he's a man who failed to suppress his passions. . . . The thing that's confusing about the Stoics is that on the one hand they say that man should be true to his nature and on the other that he should overcome his passions."

Vera put *Meditations* back on the night table.

"Well!" she said. "It doesn't look like Marcus Aurelius's made a man out of you *yet*."

"I *am* a man—in my spirit," Anna said. "Wait, and you'll see."

"Yeah? I'll see what?"

"I'll accomplish great things."

"Like what?"

"I don't know exactly—great things."

She doesn't know exactly! What bunk! Vera thought. What bunk! *She has the soul of a man. . . . She wants to kill when she is angry. . . . She hasn't hated anyone. . . .* She walked over to the window and looked out. As though anyone can keep anger and hatred apart, she thought: I hate you, but I'm not angry at you.

"You live on an unpaved street," she said.

"It's covered in cobblestone because it's old. It has historical importance, this street."

"Yes? What sort of history has it?"

"I don't know what sort. It has history."

Vera looked at the single lamppost by the churchyard.

The glass of its wrought-iron lantern looked violet in the sun. The light was beginning to pale, had a soft pink hue. She thought of the night in June she'd stood on the street corner staring at Anna across Saint John's fire.

"I'm going to go after experience—that's what I'm going to do with *my* life," Vera said.

"What do you mean, 'experience'? What do you mean, 'go after'?"

"I mean I'm going to do things to find out what it's like to do them."

"What things?"

"I don't know—things. I'm going to *live* my life."

She turned around. Anna was sitting on the edge of her bed, elbows on her open thighs.

"I have to go. I should get home before dark. The Dragon and all that . . ."

"I could wake up my father and ask him to drive you."

"No. I'm scared, but I think it's stupid. Would you be scared to walk home at this hour?"

"If I was scared, I wouldn't do it," Anna said.

"That's a new one."

"I believe that unless you're ready to die defending your life, you should lie low. Better no courage than a false show of courage. Bravado adds hypocrisy to cowardice—there's nothing more repugnant."

"Is that Marcus Aurelius?"

"It's me."

Vera rolled her eyes. "You should write it down and put it in a vault."

She put on her jacket and raised her right arm.

"Morituri te salutamus!"

Anna got up and stood motionless by her bed. A dark,

harsh light had come into her eyes. There was no discernible emotion in them, and the intensity of her stare made Vera lower her eyes. When she looked up again, Anna looked away from her.

"So go," she said. "The sooner the better."

She stood by the bed, giving no sign she intended to hug Vera good-bye.

Vera ran all the way home, unable to get the image of Anna's glowing dark eyes out of her mind. There was still plenty of light, and there were plenty of people on the streets, but her heart pounded with anxiety. She thought of the Dragon, but vaguely, as if he were no more than an idea.

INSTEAD OF starting on her homework, Anna took a photograph of Vera and herself out of the middle drawer of her desk. They were standing shoulder to shoulder, Vera with her head in profile, looking at Anna without a smile; Anna in full face, smiling widely at the lens. Behind them, in dappled sunlight and slightly out of focus, was a hedge of lilac and, to the side, on the well, a sparrow unmindfully pecking the feathers under its wing.

She looked at Vera's face but could not look at her own. She was beginning to hate her face; she cringed when she looked at herself in pictures.

What does it mean, to go after experience? she thought. What does it mean, to live one's life? There was the expression "man of experience." From what she'd seen, men of experience had bitter, worn faces, as though their knowledge of life had come from some personal defeat. There was something there she couldn't grasp. She was beginning to fear that there was something missing in her understanding. The fear

was weak—it gnawed at her as though with loose teeth—
but it filled her with great anxiety. It was as though her mind
was unequipped to understand what other people seemed
to understand instinctively and take for granted. The world
scorned you unless you had that kind of sure, shrewd understanding people called "being smart."

Smart people seemed to think the same way about things
and have the same beliefs. There was an air of complicity to
their arrogance.

Aimilia said of smart people, "They know how to exploit
life." She had a grudging admiration for smart people, as
though she'd be smart, too, if only she could.

Stephanos dismissed them. "What runs the world is not
what makes it run," he said. Anna thought that a paradox and
did not see how it pertained. For her part, all she knew was
that she could not breathe around smart people. Literally, it
made her gasp for air, and panic, as if she were pinned under
a cupping glass.

Vera was smart. She was more than just smart.

The wind was rasping against the tree branches. It had
become completely dark. The piles of books and notebooks
on her desk were in night shadow and looked grim and hateful. She loathed having to study.

She picked up the photograph again and was about to put
it back in the drawer when there was a knock on the door and
Stephanos stepped in. She jumped up from her chair and hid
the picture behind her back.

Stephanos stopped midstride and stared at her silently a
moment, then walked up close.

"Good-looking girl, your friend," he said. "You have
taste."

He went back to the door and turned the overhead lights

on. He was wearing a charcoal suit and a black turtleneck sweater. Anna noticed the brassy red highlights in his hair; it was the same deep chestnut color as her own, and she wondered if hers gave off the same glow.

"Change," he said. "I'm taking you out."

It had been months since he'd offered to take her out. They were barely on speaking terms.

"I'll wait for you in the car. We'll visit General Dimitriadis in the hospital. Wear something appropriate."

She had no idea what would be appropriate or why it should even matter. The general was in a coma.

She decided to wear the most formal thing she had, a light cashmere suit that used to be Aimilia's. It had been shortened and altered, but the jacket was still a little too long, a little too loose, and it made her body look square. She took the jacket off and went out in the suit's flattering skirt and a skintight silk top.

Stephanos was leaning against the car door, a cigarette in his hand. He took a last drag and searched his pocket for the keys.

"You need a coat or a jacket," he said.

It was freezing cold in the wind.

"I'm fine," she said, clamping her teeth.

They wouldn't have far to walk once they got to the hospital.

THE HOSPITAL had housed a high school till the war, when it had been requisitioned by the army. The wards had blackboards on the walls, gold-embossed dictums from the classics above the doors, and were filled with collapsible cots. Some rooms were numbered; some were not. Anna and

Stephanos had gone down a long corridor, come to a dead end, and were retracing their steps. The doors were open, except for one they had bypassed, taking it for a bathroom or a closet. Now they noticed the number 6, scrawled on the side frame with black paint. The inscription above the jamb was of the Delphic oracle: KNOW THYSELF.

Stephanos knocked. There was no answer. He knocked again, more gently, and opened the door.

The room had been an office. It was small and narrow, and the single bed and life-support machines took up the whole space. Stephanos and Anna had to wedge themselves in. There was a small window, but its shutters were closed and the only light came from a shaded lamp on the nightstand.

Anna could only discern outlines at first—a seemingly lifeless body under the sheets, a skeletal head with tubes coming out the nose and throat. She averted her gaze—had to force herself to look down again. The cancer had eaten into the bone. There was no jaw left and the cheeks had caved in. The mouth was a small indented hole, the lips pale and puckered like scar tissue, the nose an amorphous growth. Only the eyes were intact, shifting ceaselessly, as though unmoored in their sockets. The pupils were glazed, staring with suppliant pain. He is brain-dead, Anna thought. What was the light in his eyes—what was the anguish in them, if not experienced by the brain?

She felt horror, an unbearable sorrow. The loneliness the general had experienced his whole life suddenly seemed her own. It was every man's, every woman's and child's. The dread of knowing oneself immutably alone does not age or change, she thought. We live, we die, and we do not know why. There is nothing to allay that fact.

It now seemed so long ago, but she had been secretly in love with this man once. She had known him only a few months, but the love had stayed in her for a whole year after they parted. She'd thought of him constantly, every day; then it was as if he'd never been in her life. He never crossed her mind again.

The only reason he'd gone into the army was that his father and grandfather had been army men. He did not believe in war. It was said that in battle he shot his gun in the air, so as not to take another man's life. And yet, Anna thought, he had not avoided the risk of being killed. He had the courage to face the fire.

In conversation about the lack of women in his life, Anna had once heard a major say, "Well . . . he shoots in the air." The other officers, including her father, had laughed. They despised him and, were it not for his rank, would have openly shunned him, Anna believed.

"Doesn't he have any relatives?" she whispered. "Doesn't anyone come to see him?"

Stephanos did not answer her.

"Let's go," he said.

They had stayed only a few minutes.

When they were out in the corridor, he put his arm around her shoulders and held her a brief moment.

"I know you loved him," he said.

"Why did you despise him?" She was furious, wanted to shout the words.

"Despise him?" Stephanos said thoughtfully. "He wasn't a man I'd want in my foxhole. *Despise* is too strong. I didn't like him, but he was an honorable man."

He was honorable, Anna thought—and noble and brave. To what end? Having people snigger behind his back . . .

dying alone behind a closed door, not even a vase of flowers at his bedside.

"What people said about him—firing his gun in the air? He did not try to save his life."

"Yes, he did," he said. "He tried to save his soul."

He was silent on the way to the car. He drove staring straight ahead, both hands on the wheel, his body alert and tense.

"You and I should talk," he said.

He took her to a café, a dreary large-scale place with pale green oil-painted walls, a gray-and-black mosaic floor, and bright bare lightbulbs hanging on black cords. There was a scattering of customers—two old men playing checkers, four men playing cards, a group of merchant marines drinking ouzo, and a solitary drunk.

There were no women. He always took her places where no women went: the barber, his tailor, men's cafés—places where he should be going alone but needed company. It used to make her feel special when she was small. As at the barracks, when he took her along, the men stared and delighted over her as if she were a goldfish in a bowl. Now they stared as if she knocked the breath out of them, or with sullen resentment. Either way, it was as if her presence disturbed them, and she wanted to stay clear.

"Sit down," Stephanos said, beckoning to the waiter to come over. "What do you want to have?"

Anna gave her order to the waiter directly.

"I'd like an ouzo."

"Make that two," Stephanos said after a moment.

She had expected him to oppose her and had geared up for a fight. Now she said somewhat sheepishly, "I want to have the experience of drinking."

"Is that so," he said.

When the waiter brought their drinks, she had a sip of the ouzo, and the smell and taste disgusted her. She made a face and put down the glass.

"No," Stephanos said. "Drink it up! You said you wanted to drink ouzo, so drink ouzo."

"I wanted to know what it tasted like."

"You said you wanted to *experience* what drinking is like. Tasting is not experiencing. Tasting is affirming what you already like or dislike—tasting, you learn nothing. Drink it."

Anna raised the glass to her lips again. The taste was horrible at first, but as she kept sipping, she could not smell the licorice anymore, and the burning sensation in her throat was gone. She felt a tingling under her skin—a feathery rush of blood and heat as when she blushed. For no reason at all, she laughed.

Stephanos watched her closely.

"*That*," he said, "is experiencing."

She liked it—she loved it. It was thrilling.

"I'll tell you about drinking," he said. "The moment you start feeling the alcohol is the moment to stop."

Anna felt the alcohol but wanted to feel it more. If a little of it felt this good, more would feel all the better. She took another sip.

"You can love someone so much," she said, "you think you'll die if they don't like you back; then if you don't see them for a while, they become a stranger, as they had been before you knew them. How can love die?"

"It's not love that dies," Stephanos said. "Love does not die. Today you love this one; tomorrow you'll love that one— it's all the same love. What dies, a bit at a time, is innocence."

"I thought you didn't believe in innocence."

"I don't believe there's an innate ignorance of evil, as opposed to an innate knowledge of good. Knowledge and the capacity for evil are in us from the womb," he said. "But we're all innocent. He is innocent who is innocent of life's meaning. And that includes the priest, and that includes the cynic. Each time we stop loving, before we love anew, we get closer to life's true meaning."

"What's life's true meaning?"

"That we are alone."

"That's life's *meaning*?"

"It's a fact."

A fact is just a fact, Anna thought. It is the reason behind it that is the meaning. We are not meant to be alone. We wouldn't feel lonely if we were meant to be alone. And she did believe in an innocence that was complete ignorance of evil. A child is not surprised at a show of love, but it *is* surprised at a show of malice. An infant's eyes round out as it screams—in terror, in hurt. But she could not articulate her thoughts to him. The words did a sluggish twirl in her mouth and would not come out.

She emptied her glass.

"I'll have another one," she said.

"It will make you drunk."

"I'll have another one."

"It will make you sick. Everyone likes drinking. No one likes getting drunk."

"I'll have another one."

Stephanos ordered another round.

Anna drank the second glass faster. Each time she took a new sip, it was like stoking a fire of rage inside her. There *is* innocence, she thought. There is purity in the soul. There are those who are born with a pure soul and those who are not. She could tell when someone was pure by his eyes; there was deep kindness and a secret joy in them. She wasn't born with a pure soul herself, but she wanted to believe she could become pure—this knowing she wasn't was like a beckoning to strive. One could not feel the want of something if it did not exist.

She felt dizzy. She looked at Stephanos, and her eyesight was blurred.

"And that," he said, "is the experience of getting drunk."

He paid the bill and got up. She tried to get up, too, but her legs wobbled. She had to hold on to the table. *You can do it*, she said to herself. *You will walk*. It took the full force of her will.

Stephanos let her walk ahead of him. When they were outside, he draped his jacket over her shoulders. She turned around and faced him. "You're wrong," she said. "And another thing: I'm a woman. I'm nothing like you."

It humiliated her to slur the words, but she'd said it. She'd wanted to tell him for a long time. Now it was out.

He was silent. After a moment, he unlocked the passenger-side door and held it open for her. She got in and tried to pull the door shut, but he stopped her.

"The man opens it," he said; "the man shuts it."

He went around to the driver's side and, holding the keys in his hand, motioned to her to unlock the door. She bent over and pulled up the lock lever.

"A woman accepts a man's courtesy as his duty," he said when he got inside, "not as her due."

He checked the rearview mirror and started the engine.

"A woman does not sit with her legs open," he said.

She pulled her thighs together and held them closed tight.

"Roll down your window, or you'll get sick."

She sat still, fists clenched. As he put the car into gear, it lurched forward and everything around her seemed to swivel. She closed her eyes and saw a vortex of dark gray light, turning as though trying to unseat her mind. She had never felt so sick. It was impossible to believe she could go past this. Her stomach seemed to fold over. She retched, then tried to swallow the vomit, catching it in her hand. There wasn't much; she hadn't had any food in her stomach, and what she brought up was thin and pellucid like water but vile and bitter. Swallowing it made her gag.

Stephanos stopped the car.

"Get out and walk," he said. "You need fresh air."

They were several blocks from the house. She got out and started walking home behind the car. Her body ached as though she'd taken a beating. She felt heavy on her feet and, at the same time, oddly limber. She had no sense of time passing. One moment she had been walking behind the car, and the next she was inside the garden gate, sitting midway up the entrance stairs. She did not know how long she had been sitting there and thought she might have passed out. Her mind was alert but slow to focus, as when one is startled out of a deep sleep.

She raised her right hand, the hand she had vomited into. It stank. She put the palm to her mouth and licked it. She licked it clean—licked it till suddenly, without knowing she was doing it, her lips closed in, sucking the small mound on her palm, by the wrist. She pulled back, startled by tenderness and pleasure.

It was dark out on the street. The filament in the lantern by the churchyard was giving out and flickered rapidly, so that the dim effusion of light that reached around her seemed

like a tremor in the air. She felt as though there were someone near her, staring at her. She looked up and saw at the
bottom of the stairs, floating a quarter inch off the ground,
ghostly and luminous, the figure of the general. He was in
dress military uniform and wore his sword, but had no shoes
or hat on. His eyes stared with inconsolable despair. He
stood there for the flicker of a second and then vanished.

The light in the lantern had weakened to a steady purple
strand behind the leaded glass, and yet she could see around
her quite clearly. There was a brightness in the darkness;
even the shadows seemed to shine, as if seeped into the
ground like spilled water.

He's just died, she thought. Only the body dies and, with
the body, hope. The look in his eyes had been horrifying. It
was horrifying to realize that hope was of the body and not
of the soul—that the soul after death can only feel despair.
The body . . . she thought—the body was all one had to hold
on to.

SATURDAY WAS the eve of Vera's birthday. Anna was to spend the night and the next day before the celebration at Vera's house, they were to go to a soccer game between Panathenaikos, the Athenian team, and Aris, the Thessalonikian team.

While waiting for Anna to arrive, Vera practiced head shots in the hall with the twins' ball, throwing it up in the air and butting it toward the wall. When the bell rang, she was in a sweat. She smoothed her skirt and sweater, straightened the ribbon in her hair, refastened the bow, and jogged to the door, flick-kicking the ball across the floor.

She was out of breath when she opened the door, and she suddenly felt nervous. She was wearing a pearl-buttoned white angora sweater, a red corduroy skirt, a matching red ribbon in her hair. In the bitter cold outdoors, Anna was carrying her anorak slung over her shoulder; all she had on was a short-sleeved cotton shirt and a skimpy denim skirt. Her lips were purple, pressed tight. There were deep circles under her eyes.

"Will you let me in?" she said, pushing Vera out of the way.

She went straight to Vera's room, threw her anorak and

school bag on the bed, and plopped into the desk chair as though she owned it.

Vera took a moment to get her nerve back.

"Tremble, ye Athenians!" she said. "Prepare to be routed; fall on your knees and pray."

Anna just stared.

"Tremble, ye Athenians!" Vera said again. "Prepare to be routed; fall on your knees and pray."

"Are we going to do our homework, or what?"

"I've already done my homework. Thessalonikians study fast."

Anna looked away from her. After a moment, she got up, took her bag off the bed, unloaded the books onto the desk, and sat down with her back to the room.

Vera put her hands around her mouth and yelled, "Tremble, ye Ath—"

"If you say that one more time, I'll hit you," Anna said without turning around.

"Tremble, ye—"

Anna swiveled on the chair, knocking it down as she got up. The anger in her eyes made the rest of her face go slack, strangely tender, the lips gaping softly and trembling as though she could as easily start crying. She set the chair back on its legs and sat down again.

"Aren't you cold without a sweater?"

"I can make myself not feel the cold," Anna said.

She opened her history book and turned the pages to the following Monday's lesson. She was pale and her eyes seemed darker. There was an opaque glint over the pupils, and it was clear that though she was staring down at her book, she wasn't reading.

Vera walked to where Anna was sitting, stood behind her, and tickled her under the arms.

"Stop it."

Vera tickled harder. "Say, 'Aris is the best.' Say, 'Aris is unbeatable.'"

"Aris is the best. Stop it."

"Unbeatable . . ."

"Unbeatable."

Vera climbed on the stave between the back legs of Anna's chair and kissed her on the forehead. Anna pushed her off violently and stood up.

"Don't you have anything to do?"

"What's the matter with you?"

"Nothing is the matter with me. What would you do if I wasn't here?"

"I don't know. . . . I'd read something. . . ."

"So, read something," Anna said. She put her books back in her bag.

"What are you doing?"

"What you see I'm doing." She stood with her arms folded over her chest.

Vera took a copy of *Romance* magazine from under her mattress, threw her pillow against the headboard, and sat down on the bed, the muscles in her back tightening like a fist. She bent her knees, propped *Romance* against them, and pretended to read.

"You're going to stand there and watch me?"

Without answering her, Anna picked out a book from the bookcase and sat at the foot of the bed, her back against the wall.

"What book is that?"

"Richard the Lion-Heart."

Vera curled her lips in a sneer.

"At least I'm not reading sentimental trash," Anna said.

"At least I know I'm reading sentimental trash when I'm reading sentimental trash."

"Really. Why do you read it, then?"

"I like it."

"My point," Anna said.

"Well, you and your point can go fuck yourselves." She folded *Romance* to the page where "Love Betrayed" ran and read with peeved relish:

> Gregoris kicked the door open and loosed his buckle. She was lost! Lost to his lust! Hot bitter tears rolled down her eyes. She fell to her knees and begged, 'Don't do this! If you love the mother that brought you into the world, don't do this!' Gregoris pushed her onto the floor. . . .

The story had been running for months. If Anna was above reading *Romance*, she sure as hell was not above wanting to hear what was in it, Vera thought. Week in, week out, she had been giving Anna the lowdown on the plot. As she knew she would, after a few moments Anna asked, "What happened?"

Vera pretended not to have heard.

"What happened?"

Vera let Anna suffer a little longer, then told her. When she came to the rape scene, she filled in the dots.

"He picked up the scissors from her sewing table and raised them over her body. He began lowering them slowly— slowly down to her heart." She raised her arms, pretending she was holding the scissors, then lowered them over her chest. "He plunged them through her blouse and cut her bra off. Her breasts spilled out. He fell on top of her and put his mouth on her mouth—"

"You're making this up," Anna said. "Where does it say that?"

Vera hid *Romance* behind her back, but Anna wrestled it from her.

"You made it up," she said, skimming over the page. "I knew it!"

"So, I did."

Anna blushed, would not look Vera in the eye.

"When you read and make things up," she asked Vera after awhile, "do you pretend you are one of the characters, or do you add yourself to the plot?"

"I pretend I'm one of the characters."

"I add myself to the plot," Anna said.

"Yeah?" Vera rolled her eyes. "And who are you in *Richard the Lion-Heart*? The time-traveler damsel in distress?"

"I'm a knight," Anna said. "I fight at Richard's side, and sleep in the same tent with him at night. He does not know I'm a girl because of my armor. My voice cannot betray me, either: I'm under a vow of silence till the Grail is won."

Vera thought she'd snap. To believe Anna was to pray for disbelief sometimes. She stared at her, a silent snigger trembling on her lips.

"I often have this fantasy—winning the knight I love by proving my valor in manly disguise," Anna went on with oblivious fervor. "After I've proven my valor, I lift up my visor."

"What if it's another girl/knight you love?" Vera said. "You lift up your visor and you say, 'Ha-ha'; she lifts up her visor and she says, 'Ha-ha-*ha!*' Have you thought of that?"

"I don't say 'Ha-ha.' I kiss him. And there is no other girl/knight."

"How do you know there isn't?"

"It's my fantasy."

"Yes, well . . . your fantasy is cockeyed," Vera said. "I'm going downstairs."

She got off the bed and marched furiously to the door, but she suddenly stopped and waited.

She stood by the door.

Anna took her time getting off the bed and then followed Vera through the house and down the basement stairs, walking several steps behind.

EVERY YEAR for her birthday, Vera's godmother, who lived in Paris, sent her a gravure illustration from a classic children's book. The one for this year had arrived earlier in the month and had already been framed and put up on the playroom wall. It was a depiction of Sleeping Beauty lying on a bier of thorns, Prince Charming bent over her, the moment just before the kiss. The background and the foreground, on the sides of the bier, were filled by forest trees with human faces gnarled into the trunks and branches like outstretched arms. There was no color, just gradations of gray and black, with too narrow a strip between the treetops and matting to suggest a sky.

Anna walked up to look at it closely. In life, she thought, fear shrinks the soul; in art, it seems to make it expand in awe—a stunning, strange joy. She was amazed that a drawing so horrifying could be inextricably alloyed with beauty. To be able to see beauty in fear, what great, pure beauty must an artist feel inside him—such as no ugliness could penetrate, just as darkness cannot go into light. It was anguish to realize that she was without artistic capacity—the one thing that seemed to make living beautiful and grand. Talent was no mere ability, a honing of the will. It was a property of the soul—she could plainly see this. Artists were a different order of being.

She felt out of place in Vera's house, in the playroom especially. There were toys on shelves, a rocking horse in the corner, a low table with an electric train on it, the rails running through a papier-mâché countryside and small village. Everything looked beat-up and old—immutable since outliving its use, and with the impregnable dignity of a relic. The drab old sofa had the same forbidding dignified air, even the frayed rug. The whole room seemed sealed in childhood's past.

She walked back to the card table and sat down opposite Vera, between the twins.

"Take the red," Vera said. "I left you the red."

It was the color Anna always chose. She looked down at the Monopoly board.

"Do I hear 'thank you'?" Vera said.

"Thank you once," said Fotis.

"Thank you twice," said Nikitas.

They were wearing matching blue sweaters, but Fotis wore a white shirt under his.

"We have no bidder," he said.

"Let's start already," Vera said.

They threw the dice to decide the starting order. It came out Vera, Anna, Fotis, and Nikitas. Vera landed in jail. Anna picked up a card that sent her back to Go.

"A 'still start,' you might say," Fotis said.

"Play," Vera said to him.

Fotis slid down in his chair, raised his right knee above the edge of the table, and twisted his right arm under his thigh. He shook the dice in his fist.

"That's how they do it in Las Vegas," he said.

He sat up straight again. He kept jiggling the dice. "Hermes Road . . ." he whispered. "Hermes Road . . . Hermes—"

"Throw the dice," Vera said.

Fotis blew into his cupped fist.

"Oh, throw the damn dice and be done with it!" Vera screamed.

He landed on Hermes Road.

"What did I say?" he said. "What did I say?"

"Play!" Vera screamed at Nikitas.

"Is she on the rag?" Fotis stage-whispered. "Hey, Veronica, are you on the rag? Anna, darling. Cheer up your friend. She hurts."

"Cheer up," Anna said uncomfortably.

"You should hire your services out," Nikitas said.

"The cheering maiden—"

"The jester in skirts."

"Anna, will you be my fool?" Fotis got out of his chair, fell on his knees, and pressed his palms together in prayerlike entreaty. "Anna, will you cheer me?"

Vera banged her fists on the table, sending the Monopoly board to the floor.

"Idiots!" she shrieked. "Idiots!" She got up. "I'm going to my room," she said. But she did not move.

Fotis got up on his feet.

They were all silent a moment. From the kitchen upstairs

came the sound of pots and pans being set down and moved about, the sweeping *whoosh* of scurrying feet.

"Why don't we start over?" Anna said.

"Yes," Vera said with scathing coldness. "Why don't you start over?"

She left the room. Anna could hear her footsteps, slow, banging with fury on the stairs.

Fotis remained standing, looking at her from the corner of his eye. Nikitas stared at her, his pupils dark, the irises wide, a blank yet tense expression on his face. His sweater gaped at the neck and his naked skin glowed in the faint electric light like a tremor she wished she could still.

"I'm going up, too," she said.

They didn't say anything to her, just kept staring.

"I'll see you later," she said.

She started to walk away. Still, they did not say anything. Each step she took, she was aware of having to lift her foot. When she was out of the room, she gasped for air. She didn't know why she was so anxious.

When she walked into the room, Vera was sitting at her vanity, brushing her hair with furious strokes. She had tossed her red ribbon onto the floor.

Anna sat on the bed. The curtains were drawn and the glass in the windows reflected the room but not the place where she sat. It was black outside, though the clock on the nightstand read only a quarter to seven.

DINNER WAS FINISHED, but the Koroneous lingered at the table and, as the guest, Anna could not get up and leave first. She was edgy with boredom and with that particular anxiety that came over her just before going to bed. Dinner had been unusually silent. Only Vera's parents, Vera, and herself were present. The twins had gone to the movies, and Christophoros—whom Anna had not seen all evening—was going out with friends. He appeared at the doorway, wearing a black leather jacket, gloves in his hand.

"I'm going," he said. "I'm taking the car."

He glanced at Anna absently, then seemed startled. He stared at her a long moment; then, neither greeting her nor smiling, he turned around and walked out without saying good night to anyone.

He wanted to get away from her as fast as he could, Anna thought. He never tried to talk to her. Each time she saw him, he was less civil—staring her straight in the face as if she was supposed to smile first. It was humiliating that she liked him.

"Out on the prowl," Vera said. "But we nice girls stay in our nest." She got up and stretched.

"Anna, my child," Mando said, "you look peaked. Are you feeling well?"

"I'm fine."

"She's in roaring good health," Dr. Koroneou said with a wry smile. "She ate with a wolf's appetite. She has room left over to eat us, too, but she's too polite."

"Don't you listen to him," Mando said.

She was dressed beautifully tonight, in a tight jersey dress that made her breasts stretch the cloth as though they were about to burst.

"Good night, my child," she said.

"Good night," Anna said, blushing.

"You sleep in or out?" Vera asked when they were back in her room.

"Out."

Turning toward the window, she listened to the low, moaning whine of the car engine as Christophoros drove off. There was no other traffic.

Vera pulled down the covers.

"Have you brought a nightgown?"

"I don't own a nightgown. I hate them. They ride up the legs and strangle you while you sleep."

"They strangle you. . . ."

"Haven't you ever woken up in the middle of the night with your nightgown twisted up like a noose?"

"No . . . But danger lurks everywhere, I'm sure."

"I'm serious," Anna said. "I sleep in the nude."

Vera reeled back. "Not next to me you don't!"

Before Anna had the chance to add that she intended to keep her underwear on, Vera rushed out of the room, leaving Anna standing with her mouth open. She came back a few minutes later, walking in a surly strut, two sets of pajamas over her outstretched arms.

"For me, for you."

They turned their backs to each other and changed.

The pajamas were of heavy flannel and had blue and white vertical stripes. They were much too big.

"They might look better if we put the tops on backward," Vera said.

They buttoned each other in the back.

"Now we look like convicts," Vera said.

"Condemned men," Anna said excitedly, "like—"

"Yes! In the Bastille!"

They butted heads and grinned. They had both read *Les Misérables*.

"We have to dig ourselves out of here. We have to make a tunnel through the floor," Vera said.

They fell on their knees and pretended to dig. Just then, Mando walked in, carrying a tray with two glasses and a pitcher of water.

"You lost something?" she said.

Anna stood up, embarrassed.

"Beastly jailer!" Vera said, glaring at her mother. "Traitor to France! Torturer! The time for retribution has come."

"You shouldn't sit on the floor in your sleep clothes," Mando answered. "Who told you to wear your brothers' things?"

Vera stood up and put her arm around Anna's shoulders. She started singing "La Marseillaise" in full cry:

> *"Allons enfants de la patrie,*
> *Le jour de gloire est arrivé*
>
> *"Tata tata tatatata*
> *Tata tata tatatata"*

"You're disturbing the neighbors. Stop it." Mando's face had a flushed and bloated look, as if she were holding her breath, trying not to explode.

There was no menace to her anger—it was like rage that has no recourse but resentment. Anna was crushed to see the creases around her mouth—which rippled with gentleness when she smiled—turn harsh and bitter. Hard, if fleeting, a glint of malice had shown in her eyes. Anna had believed Mando was nice. She had been ready to apologize. But she would never apologize to a person with a streak of meanness.

"I want you to know that I'm stopping because I don't know the other verses," Vera said. "The cry of freedom cannot be silenced."

Mando shut a gaping bureau drawer, folded up the skirt, sweater, slip, and bra that Vera had flung over her desk, and left, slamming the door.

Vera rummaged in the top shelf of the closet and brought out two white balloons.

"We need balls and chains," she said. "Blow them up. I'll go fetch some string. We'll tie them to our ankles."

Anna had lost interest. It all felt so silly suddenly. When she lived out a fantasy, it was as if she had been taken by force. It was spontaneity precisely that made a fantasy realer than life. This now was like mounting a show. But Vera had gotten even more fired up since Mando left, and, sheepishly, Anna went along, blowing air into the balloons.

"It has to be hand to hand and foot to foot," Vera said, passing her a piece of string.

"I believe a chain gang is foot to foot only."

"No," Vera said. "It's hand *and* foot."

She demonstrated a knot she had learned in Girl Scouts.

"No-no-no-no! *Over*loop," she said as Anna tried to tie the balloon to her leg. "No-no-no-no! *Under*loop."

She was so eager and frustrated, she made Anna break into a sweat. The string kept slipping out of her hands.

"Oh, why don't I just do you." She tied the balloon to Anna's leg; then she tied her left hand to Anna's right hand, wrist bone to wrist bone.

"There's supposed to be a chain length linking the hand-cuffs," Anna said.

"We're Siamese twins."

"I thought we were convicts."

"Siamese twin convicts," Vera said.

She bent down to tie their legs together, lost her balance, and fell down, trampling and bursting the balloons.

"You should have done the legs first," Anna told her.

"Oh, why don't you shut up. Bend over and give me some help."

They managed to tie their feet together—anklebone to anklebone, without slack.

"Now what?" Anna said.

They stood up, pushing against the edge of the bed for leverage.

"Now . . ." Vera said, "now . . ."

They burst out laughing. They couldn't stop. Each time they tried holding their breath, the laughter came back stronger.

"I have to go pee," Anna said. "It's from laughing—"

"Me, too."

"Untie us! Untie us! Fast!"

They could not untie the knots.

"We'll have to go like this," Vera said.

They clambered out to the hall, at first hopping on their bound feet, then lowering themselves to the floor and creeping on their stomachs. When they got to the bathroom, they staggered back up to their feet, only to realize that the toilet was set too tight between the wall and the sink and there was not enough room for the one to sit and the other to stand at the side.

"The tub," Vera said. "Squat over the tub."

She took a step forward, but too hastily, and slipped on the mat, falling on her back and pulling Anna on top of her. They started to laugh again, convulsed with quiet, stifled sobs. Anna felt a small amount of urine uncontrollably escape.

"You peed on me," Vera screamed. "You—" But she peed, too. Piss gushed out of her onto Anna's thigh.

Anna let herself go, too. They lay still, their bodies slack from hard laughter, the warm piss cooling fast, a feeling of numbness spreading between them. Distant and soft, then louder and sharp like crackling ice, the solitary footsteps of a person walking down the street echoed through the house, then vanished.

"The Dragon . . ." Vera whispered.

Her voice was hoarse with fear. She held her breath, then started breathing shallowly and fast, her chest heaving into Anna's chest with each breath. Anna did not feel any fear. If it was the Dragon, he had passed by the house. Vera's terrified breathing made her feel a violent, thrilling, uncontrollable emotion—totally confusing, like cruelty, but not hateful. Clamping her thighs around Vera's thigh, she clasped her shoulder, relishing the pain as the string cut into her wrist as though it were pleasure. She squeezed harder, digging her nails in. Her whole body trembled.

"Get off of me," Vera said, suddenly dead calm. "Get off, I tell you."

She looked at Anna with horror and disgust. She looked at her as if at a bug she was too squeamish to squash.

HER SENSES still muddled with sleep, Vera could hear heavy rain pounding on the roof. Water gushed down the drainpipe on the other side of the wall and the shutters shook from the wind like chattering teeth. The first thought in her mind, as though she'd dreamed it, was of a dog her family had kept when she was a small child. She did not know exactly what breed it was—a big hunting dog with floppy ears and a reddish coat. Its owner—she did not remember who its owner was, either, some friend of her father's—had gone on a trip to Europe. The dog refused food and drink. All night, all day, day after day, it lay in the same spot by the garden gate and howled. It did not let up till its strength started giving out, and then it whimpered with its eyes shut. When its master came back, it could barely stand up. The first thing it did was pee. It was a bitch, and it squatted, teetering on its hind legs, and while it peed, it weakly wagged the tip of its tail.

She had this memory often, and always when she did, she felt raw and fresh the despair she'd felt listening to the dog howl, thinking that its horrifying misery was what love did to those who loved truly, deeply.

Anna lay on her stomach near the edge of the bed, one arm over her head, the other hanging down, her face turned away. She was breathing evenly and quietly, but her body had tensed when Vera had sat up. Vera knew she was awake. She whispered, "Anna . . ." and again, louder, not wanting to touch her, "Anna . . ."

It was seven o'clock. Everyone would still be asleep. Vera crawled to the foot of the bed, straddled the footboard, and climbed down. She didn't want to stay in her room—she didn't want to be in there one minute longer.

She went to the living room and turned the radio on. Programs One and Two were carrying the early Sunday liturgy. Program Three was broadcasting a talk on tradition in Greek music.

"Pontian music derives directly from the music of the ancient Greeks," the announcer said. "The following song celebrates the victory of battle."

Vera lay on the couch and closed her eyes. The song had the melody of a syncopated drone, she thought. The male singers sang with high-pitched, squealing voices, as if someone were squeezing their balls. If that was a Greek chant of victory, she'd have to abjure her race.

The rain was coming down harder. There was no doubt the soccer game would be canceled. It was her birthday, and she was sitting here all alone, up since dawn, wanting to kill herself for nothing better to do. Maybe she could paint her toenails—that's what she should do. Bright red, for her birthday.

She tiptoed into her parents' bedroom, took a bottle of nail varnish and some cotton out of Mando's vanity, and returned to the living room. The music program was over and "Advice to Our Farmers" had come on. She sat down on the floor, put swabs of cotton between her toes, and painted her toenails while listening to a lecture on the perils of fruit flies.

"Fruit flies and early frost are a citrus grower's nemesis," the commentator concluded. "One can be fought against; the other is prey to the vagaries of fate."

It was a sight she'd like to see—a farmer glued to the radio, nodding in appreciation and gratitude for the advice: Yield to vagaries of fate; fight fruit flies.

What bunk! she thought. What bunk!

She heard someone go into the bathroom, then come out. She wanted to call out, "I'm in here," but she stopped herself. They can hear the radio; they should come looking for me, she thought. It was her birthday, after all.

She waited.

Her toenails looked pretty. She had done a perfect job.

She could hear her parents' voices in the kitchen. No sound of anyone coming to find her.

Oh, the hell with it. She stared at her feet and started to

sob. She did not know why she was crying. She didn't feel grief. Yet, when she stopped, an unbearable pain welled up. She wanted to crawl back into bed. She wanted the day to go away. She wanted Anna to hold her under the covers—and keep still.

But when she went back to her room, her bed was empty. Anna's clothes and her school bag were gone. On the desk was a long, narrow gift-wrapped box and a note written on a torn notebook page. She snatched the note and read it: "I've gone home. Happy birthday, A."

She tore up the gift wrap and opened the box with shaking hands. Inside, couched in blue velvet, was a letter opener, the blade wide and curving slightly at the tip, the hilt carved with a filigree of flowers and leaves. She took it out and held it by the blade. There was black tarnish in the indentations of the hilt. She ran her fingers over the smooth, delicate ridges of the leaves, though she knew they'd stain. A knife that didn't cut . . .

MONDAY MORNING, as Vera turned a corner on her way to school, she saw Anna walking a few paces ahead. She sneaked up behind her and put her hands over Anna's eyes.

"Guess who?"

Anna tried to push her off, but Vera held tight. "I'm the Big Bad Wolf," she whispered, sinking her teeth into Anna's neck. "I'm going to eat you—eat you—eat you."

"It tickles," Anna said. Her face was still swollen with sleep and her voice was husky and deep.

"You taste salty," Vera said, letting go. "Like roasted peanuts."

Anna glared at her, then resumed walking, weaving

sleepily from side to side. She bumped into Vera every other step.

"Stop bumping me," Vera said.

Anna blushed and started walking faster, with an angry stomping gait.

"It was a rotten thing not to stay for my birthday."

Anna did not answer. Vera slowed down and let her walk ahead, but, after a few steps, Anna stopped and waited for her with her head down.

"Look at me!" Vera said.

Anna looked away.

Vera walked in front of her and grabbed her by the shoulders. "Look at me!"

Anna stared, her pupils glazed over. She pushed Vera's hands away.

"We'll be late," she said. But she walked on slowly, suddenly dragging her feet.

It was sunny and bright, though a cluster of dark clouds was drifting inland from over the sea. Vera was cold; the earth was still damp from yesterday's downpour.

"Aren't you cold?"

Anna did not answer.

By the time they reached school, assembly was over and the custodian had locked the gate. He gave them lateness slips and sent them to the principal's office.

As they turned the corridor corner, they came face-to-face with a short, bowlegged woman. Her hair was short, grease-slicked, and combed back, her face broad, with a square jaw. She had immense jutting breasts and walked chest out, like a figure on a ship's prow. She stared Anna in the eyes as she passed by, then gave Vera a fleeting glance.

"Who was *that*?" Vera whispered.

"She looked at me as though she knew me," Anna said.

"A Quasimodo with the hump in front—that's what she looked like."

They knocked on Athanasiades' door.

"Enter!"

He looked at their lateness slips, acting crestfallen.

"Karystinou! Koroneou!" he said. "You're both excellent students. It pains me deeply to give you a demerit."

He straightened some papers on his desk, read over a letter, signed it, and took off his glasses.

"It pains me very deeply," he repeated. "What excuse do you have to give me?"

"We have no excuse," Anna said.

"Does that mean you're sorry?"

Vera lowered her eyes, trying to look repentant.

"It means we have no excuse," Anna said flatly.

"One demerit for being late, two demerits for being impertinent, and you are to stand at attention out in the hall till recess." He picked up the ledger and searched for their names. "You may leave."

"Are you crazy?" Vera said as they walked to the end of the hall. "Are you insane? Three demerits means 'bad conduct' on our reports. You should have said we were sorry."

"I don't grovel and I don't lie."

"Speak for yourself alone next time."

"I shall."

"You have this on your conscience. Remember that!"

"I shall."

"Next time you don't want to grovel and lie, let me know in advance."

"I shall."

Vera stuck out her tongue. "I shall—I shall—I shall." She

sat down on the windowsill. Anna leaned against the wall. Till the bell rang, they did not say another word.

PUNISHMENT upon punishment, Vera thought. She had endured detention in the hall; now she had to endure religion class. As was his wont, Varnalis entered the classroom at his the-hour-is-nigh gallop. Instead of the usual gray suit, he was wearing a light blue sweater. It lit up his face, for all the difference it made. He was long-necked and held his head forward like a goose.

"Matthew twenty-five, verses fourteen through thirty," he said. He waited for the rustle of turning pages to end and then started to read:

"For the kingdom of heaven is as a man traveling into a far country, who called his own servants, and delivered unto them his goods.

"And unto one he gave five talents, to another two, and to another one; to every man according to his several ability; and straightway took his journey.

"Then he that had received the five talents went and traded with the same, and made them other five talents.

"And likewise he that had received two, he also gained other two.

"But he that had received one went and digged in the earth, and hid his lord's money.

"After a long time the lord of those servants cometh, and reckoneth with them.

"And so he that had received five talents came and brought other five talents, saying, Lord, thou deliveredst unto me five talents: behold, I have gained beside them five talents more.

"His lord said unto him, Well done, good and faithful servant: thou hast been faithful over a few things, I will make thee ruler over many things: enter thou into the joy of thy lord.

"He also that had received two talents came and said, Lord, thou deliveredst unto me two talents: behold, I have gained two other talents beside them.

"His lord said unto him, Well done, good and faithful servant; thou hast been faithful over a few things, I will make thee ruler over many things: enter thou into the joy of thy lord.

"Then he which had received the one talent came and said, Lord, I knew thee that thou art an hard man, reaping where thou hast not sown, and gathering where thou hast not strawed:

"And I was afraid, and went and hid thy talent in the earth: lo, there thou hast that is thine.

"His lord answered and said unto him, Thou wicked and slothful servant, thou knewest that I reap where I sowed not, and gather where I have not strawed:

"Thou oughtest therefore to have put my money to the exchangers, and then at my coming I should have received mine own with usury.

"Take therefore the talent from him, and give it unto him which hath ten talents.

"For unto everyone that hath shall be given, and he shall have abundance: but from him that hath not shall be taken away even that which he hath.

"And cast ye the unprofitable servant into outer darkness: there shall be weeping and gnashing of teeth."

"What is a talent?" he said.

Vera raised her hand, but Varnalis called on Anna. He

always looked to Anna for the answer when he wanted to make a point, as if they were in cahoots. Vera loathed him for it.

"It was the monetary unit of the time," Anna said.

"Talents stand for talents," Vera said under her breath.

"Koroneou, you want to enlighten us, speak up!"

Vera was silent.

"Karystinou, I'm asking again: What is a talent?"

"The ability to do something," Anna said.

"Like walk," Vera muttered.

"I heard you, Koroneou," Varnalis said. "Talent is an effortless propensity to excellence in some field. It's a manifestation of God's grace. . . . The unprofitable servant said, 'And I was afraid, and went and hid thy talent in the earth.' What was he afraid of? What was the risk? To lose all he had. But was it his, what he had? How can we lose what we don't own—what belongs to God?"

"Go tell that to Job," Vera said under her breath, but loud enough to be heard.

Varnalis ignored the remark. "We lose an ability by not using it. There's risk only in taking no risk."

"Like the gambler says . . ." Vera said.

"You have another sarcastic remark, Koroneou, stand up and make it. Don't hide your darkness under a bushel."

Vera stood up. "The unprofitable servant was afraid because the lord made him feel unworthy," she said. "He gave him just one talent, as if that was all he was good for."

"You think you're smart, do you?"

"Yes, I do."

"Let's have it in writing. I want you to go to the

blackboard and write ten times in capital letters: 'Vera Koroneou thinks she's smart.' "

Vera went to the blackboard and began to write: 1. VERA KORONEOU IS SMART. 2. VERA KORONEOU IS SMART. 3. VERA KORONEOU IS SMART. . . .

"There's no one unworthy in the eyes of the Lord but the proud," Varnalis said to the class. He turned to Vera. "I said to write, '*thinks* she's smart,' " he said. "Erase the blackboard and write, 'Vera Koroneou *thinks* she's smart.' A hundred times this time."

It took Vera longer than the class period. When the bell rang, she was down on her knees, scrawling line 76.

"Erase the top lines and continue during recess," Varnalis told her as he left the classroom.

When everyone had walked out, Anna went up to her and stood by.

"I'm sorry," she said.

"Yeah? What for?"

Anna avoided her eyes. "That was a good answer," she said.

"As you declared, standing up for me—so the whole class could hear."

Anna blushed.

"I'm sorry. . . . I'm sorry. . . . I'll wait for you here."

"You can go to hell," Vera said.

It took everything she had not to start crying.

ANNA FELT AWFUL about herself. All day, she'd been angry at Vera—wanted her out of her sight. She treated Anna one moment as if she liked her, the next as if she wanted to crush her with her heel like a worm. She couldn't stand it anymore. There'd been a part of her that had been pleased, seeing Vera brought low. Yet, but for that appalling tinge of vindication and glee, seeing her on her knees, the hurt had been worse than if she'd been humiliated herself. I love her, she thought. I love her! Only love could cause such wrenching shame and guilt. It was impossible to exonerate betrayal, not standing up to defend a friend, but she would do penance—she'd humble herself. If Vera gave her another chance, she'd show her the love she felt—she'd prove it to her.

She waited for Vera in the yard. The bell had rung, and gym class was about to start, but Vera had not come down.

It was cold. The cloud mass was swelling and darkening. There was still a hazy gray aura of sunlight, but the air was already dense with the dampness of the oncoming storm. The girls were scattered through the yard, dressed in cotton shorts and T-shirts, shivering. There was no sign of the teacher. Some girls started heading back toward the changing room in the basement. Just as Anna decided to join them, Athanasiades and the woman she had seen earlier that morning in the hall walked into the yard and mounted the podium.

Athanasiades waved the girls who were leaving back into the yard. "Miss Romanou had to leave the school for family reasons," he said. "Your new gym teacher for the rest of the year will be Miss Stamatia Trita."

He stepped down, watched the girls gather in formation, then walked back up the stairs with stooped shoulders and head.

"Sing 'Greece Never Dies.' March!" Trita commanded in a booming deep voice.

She was standing chin out. As Anna stared at her, she met

her eyes and held her glance steady and fierce, as though daring her to take a swing.

Anna was unsettled. What was that about?

There was still no sign of Vera. As Anna marched, she
kept looking back toward the door of the changing room.
She felt Trita staring at her and became even more tense. She
kept stumbling, missing the beat. The class should be dismissed, she thought. It had begun to drizzle; it was freezing.
She turned her head and looked furiously at Trita. What are
you trying to prove? her glance said. She *would* swing at her
if she could. She was mean—she was repulsive. Each new
time she missed the beat, she turned and looked at Trita defi-
antly. After a while, Trita's ugliness seemed to gain a compelling force. It wasn't defiance anymore; Anna couldn't take
her eyes off her. She was losing the beat entirely.

The march song ended and the column came to a stop. It
had begun to rain.

"Go on," Trita said. She took out her whistle and blew on
it a one-two marching beat.

She's a sadist, Anna thought. A bully. But she had to force
herself not to keep looking at the teacher. To keep her mind
off her, she started to write out in her head the composition
assignment Prokopiou had given the class for the following
Monday. "In fairy tales," she had said, "a central metaphor
transfers the meaning of something that is abstract and thus
defuses emotional response to something concrete that can
elicit a specific feeling. The theme is: 'Why popular imagination has seized on the name Dragon for the serial killer.' I
want you to examine: What is a dragon? What does he stand
for?"

In fairy tales, the dragon breathes fire. He protects a cave
where there is a hidden treasure. There is always a princess

and a prince. Sometimes, the princess knows what will kill the dragon and tells the prince. Sometimes, the princess is inside the cave, tied in chains. The prince always wins. The dragon always is slain. The princess always marries the prince. Anna could not see the metaphor. What was the treasure? Why was the dragon guarding it? What was his loyalty? He died of it—honorably, though a mere beast.

Lost in thought, she slowed down, backing into the girl who was marching in the row behind. She did a polka step and a hop, a polka step and a hop, but she couldn't get back in step.

"*Left* right, *left* right," Trita yelled, marching up close and practically screaming into Anna's ear.

Anna blushed. Her legs jerked forward as though she were a spastic. The harder she tried to keep to the beat, the more she went off it.

"Halt!" Trita said. "Face left!"

The column became four deep and a dozen long.

Trita spread her legs apart and put her hands on her waist. "You," she said. "What is your name?"

"Anna Karystinou."

"Anna Karystinou, what?"

The rain was coming down harder. Anna felt it pelting her head, watched it splatter on Trita's white shirt, making it transparent over her huge breasts. She could see the delineation of her bra, two curling shadows at the place of the nipples.

"Anna Karystinou, Miss Trita," she said.

"Three steps forward!"

Anna stepped out of the ranks.

"Which is your left leg?"

Anna pointed.

"Which is your right leg?"

Anna pointed to her right leg.

"Do you know how to walk?"

Even with the cold rain splashing on her skin, Anna could feel the heat of blood rushing to her face.

"I'm waiting for an answer."

"Yes."

" 'Yes, I know how to walk, Miss Trita,' is what you say. You speak in full sentences when addressing a teacher."

"Yes, I know how to walk, Miss Trita."

"March around the yard."

Anna was incredulous. She did not move, thinking it had to be a joke. Trita turned around and dismissed the class. Anna watched the girls stampede toward the building, wondering if the dismissal was meant to include her, but she stayed where she was.

"March around the yard till I tell you to stop," Trita commanded, turning to her again.

She had lowered her voice when she spoke and its steady, quiet tone had been taunting and intimate. Her mouth was soft around the edges, the lips slack, rain-streaked, purple from the cold. There were creases on them—deep and firm, like wrinkles of grief, and Anna, feeling a cowering, confusing tenderness, obeyed.

She had walked more than half the circumference of the yard when the "till I tell you to stop" hit her with its full demeaning force. She stopped, rigid with sudden, overwhelming rage. She felt a hatred so deep, so hideous, her whole body writhed and trembled with it.

They stood at a standstill, the rain beating on them relentlessly. After a while, Trita walked away, but Anna remained standing in the rain.

VERY EARLY Thursday morning, less than a week after the last murder, the Dragon had struck again. There were two victims, both nineteen years old, roommates he surprised in their sleep. One had been killed with the single crushing blow over the left temple that was his mark; the other had put up a fight and bore several contusions over the head and chest but had survived and was in a coma.

Anna was about to leave for the bookstore to exchange *Moby Dick* for another book when she heard a new news bulletin come on the radio. She went to the living room to listen. It was early evening and in the bleary dusk light coming through the windows, her parents, sitting on opposite ends of the sofa, were tense shadowy figures, silent and remote. There was no new information; it was an exact repetition of the earlier bulletin—senseless words strung together like notes making up melody in music, a bleak refrain of the same song. Nothing made sense anymore.

She turned the overhead lights on, watched her parents start and look up a moment, then continue to listen, heads bent.

"I'm going to the bookstore to return a book."

She expected them to make a fuss about her going out in the dark alone, and she had geared up for a fight, but they did not say a word. Without the barb of defiance to latch on to, her resolve to go gave way.

"If I see a man with a bloodied stone in his hand, I'll cross to the other side of the road."

"That's not a joke," Aimilia said.

Stephanos stared at her through the cloud of cigarette smoke. "You're dawdling," he said. "If you're going to go, go."

To stay, at this point, would make her look a fool.

It was darker outside than she had thought. When she got to the main street, she walked close to the lighted stores, hugging the wall. Several men went past, giving her lewd glances and walking on purposefully and fast. There were no other women out, not that she could see. She felt naked in her skirt, alone among all these men. Each time a car drove by, it lit her up. It was like having to run a gauntlet just to get to a store. But the thought of the waiting books calmed her somewhat.

Looking at life firsthand, whatever understanding she gleaned, an opposite understanding came around and stabbed her in the back. Only books could impart knowledge one could trust. When reading a book, she could say, Yes, that's true, and no matter how horrifying the thing was, the certainty of its truth did away with the fear. To understand is to feel the mind go calm, she thought. If there were nothing left to understand, there would be nothing left to fear. She was going to make it her aim to understand everything there was to understand.

There were no other customers when she walked in. Aryeres, the owner's son, was standing behind the counter opposite the door, reading the extra edition of *The Greek North*.

"If she comes out of it, she'll be able to give a description," Anna said.

"If . . ." he said.

He was eighteen years old, muscular and broad-shouldered, with a worn-down look. He went to school and worked at the store weekends and nights. His soft gray eyes became brilliant and dark when he spoke with emotion. Anna had never known anyone whose eyes changed so sharply. There was something unsettling about it. He had the brooding intensity of someone utterly self-centered, and when he focused on another person, it was with an air of impatience and condescension. Nevertheless, Anna liked him: He knew what he was talking about, and despite his rough and surly manner, he was not above showing respect when it was due. He was nice to her.

"You didn't like it?" he said, taking *Moby Dick* back to the stacks.

"I couldn't get into it. If I wanted to read about whale hunting, I would have asked you for a fishing manual."

"I misjudged you," he said. "*Moby Dick* is a great book."

He misjudged the book, she thought. It was so long-winded and verbose, she'd heaved sighs trying to develop an interest.

"I thought I was reading a sermon on sea adventure," she told him.

"Well . . ." he scoffed. "It's a sea adventure that's only the greatest allegory about man's confrontation with evil ever written."

She hadn't even remotely seen that. Perhaps she hadn't read far enough.

"I hate allegories. When I read something, I like to know

what I'm reading. I don't want to have to guess at some hidden intended meaning."

Unlike the arguments she had with Vera, a difference of opinion with Aryeres left no hard feelings, but added to the excitement of being with each other. She loved disagreeing with him, though something in her made her hold back from totally speaking her mind, and she kept her best ace up her sleeve. With Vera, she played her aces up front, as if she wanted the game called off—done with.

"Is that so?" he said.

"That is so."

He went to the back of the store to look for another book for her.

"I don't want some mushy love story, either," she called after him.

After her first few purchases, he had flatly refused to sell her the abridged-for-children novels her parents made her ask for and pushed instead what he called "serious literature." That had turned out to be novels with brainy, destitute heroines who eked out their living as governesses or boarding-school teachers, while pining for the love of some arrogant, well-heeled man. She had to put her foot down to get anything else.

He came back carrying a wide-spined maroon-covered book that looked to be a thousand pages long. He put it on the counter, laid his hands over the cover, and leaned slightly forward. His body seemed to be held weightless by the soft light. She could see, through the frayed weave of his sweater, the bulge of tight muscles on his shoulder. His forearms were bare, the sleeves bunched up just below the elbow.

"Where is your father tonight?" she asked.

"Out."

He avoided her eyes and looked down at the counter.

"It scares you how big it is?" he said.

She didn't know what he meant. His voice had a changed, softer tone. She felt intensely uncomfortable; then, as he lifted his hands from the cover, she realized he meant the book, but the discomfort didn't go away, and she looked down at the book to hide her face.

It was titled *The Idiot*, with letters embossed in gold leaf and fashioned in the Byzantine script used for ecclesiastical texts.

"What is it about?"

"The idea that pure goodness cannot exist in this world without being destroyed."

"Only an idiot would want to be good—is that the message?"

"Put in one sentence . . ."

She flipped the back cover open. The book was 856 pages long. Just holding it in her hands was daunting.

"You'll like it," he said.

She looked on the flyleaf for the price. It was much more than *Moby Dick* cost.

"I don't want the extra money," he said, as though reading her mind. "I want you to have this book. It's my gift. You can exchange *Moby Dick* for another book next time."

She hesitated. Her father said, "One should refuse an uncalled-for gift." He said, "One should not accept a favor one cannot return."

"Take it," Aryeres said. "I think of you as a friend."

His eyes were shining. She could see—there was no mistaking it—there was love, pure love, in his eyes.

Her father said, "The man who pretends to be a woman's friend is a wolf in a sheep's pelt." He said, "What to a woman is friendship, to a man is patience while he lays out his snare." He said, "The Devil does not hit anyone over the head to make him go his way; he smiles and appears to be kind, generous, and honest." He said, "If a man tries to sell you love, tell him to go have his grist ground at another mill. He'll know what you mean."

He doesn't have to know, she thought. She wanted to cry, she felt so torn.

"If you wait around till I close, I'll walk you home," Aryeres said.

"No, no, no—I have to go!"

She bolted out of the store. She didn't even realize she'd taken the book along till she was halfway down the block. She pressed *The Idiot* over her heart, repeating anxiously in her mind, It's my gift. I want it. . . . It's mine. I can have it. . . . She was oblivious to everything around her. It was only when she was right near her house that she noticed how dark and empty the street was. She was terrified. She had let her mind slip. The Dragon could appear from anywhere, and she'd let her mind slip.

ANNA STARTED *The Idiot* that night, after everyone had gone to sleep. She was immediately, completely immersed: She was in the train of the opening scene; she saw the passengers; she saw the foggy light. She had to read slowly because the writing was dense, and yet it was as though she were hearing a live voice telling her the story. No word got jammed between her mind and ear.

As when she daydreamed, she was not aware of time. Suddenly, her eyes hurt and she was stunned to realize, looking at the clock, that it was past five in the morning. She did not want to let the book go. Reading it had been making her feel a joy inseparable from awe. Only one other thing had made her feel this way.

One day, when she was nine and living with her grandparents, the sun had seemed to shine unusually bright. It was early morning, spring, and she was on her way to school, walking through an empty lot strewn with poppies. She stopped walking, her body utterly still with joy—with sudden terror. She was still a believer in those days and constantly prayed to Jesus. The beauty of the light was His presence, she thought. It was His love, the stunning joy in her soul. He had heard her prayers—had come to let her know He listened. For days after, whenever the light was soft and beautiful, as at dusk or in the early morning, she believed Jesus would appear to her again, this time taking form. She started praying to Him to give her first a sign—make a voice in her mind say, Now! If He appeared too suddenly, she was sure she would die of fright. The terror of anticipation became far greater than her joy. In the end, whenever the light shone brightly and joy sprang in her heart, she shut her eyes and denied Him.

SHE SLEPT through the alarm the next morning. When Aimilia came in to rouse her, she was too exhausted to get up.

"Leave me alone—I'm sick," she told her. "My stomach hurts."

It was the first outright lie she'd told, and instantaneously her stomach cramped and did hurt, as though to make truth of her words. The pain was bad, but she was able to drift back to sleep, and she did not wake up again till noon.

"You shouldn't have cocoa," Aimilia told her when she walked into the kitchen. "Have some chamomile tea."

She had been chopping onions and her face was flushed, tears rolling down her cheeks. She moved the knife up and down with a jerky, vehement motion, as if the onion were vermin trying to skitter away.

"Why?" She hated chamomile tea.

"It settles the stomach."

Anna had forgotten all about her hurting stomach.

"I'm better now."

"Even so. Sit down. I'll make you a cup."

Anna sat at the table and waited.

"I'm hungry."

"You can have some plain toast."

Anna bowed her head. She was ravenous. She devoured the single piece of toast but did not touch the tea.

"If Vera calls later, I'll be in my room."

"I'll make a note of that," Aimilia said.

Shut in her room, she read all afternoon. She broke for supper, when mercifully she was allowed to eat, and went back to reading. She read into the night again.

When she went to bed Saturday night, she was only a few pages from the end, the point where Rogozhin pulls the curtain to show Myshkin the corpse of Nastassya Filippovna. Sunday, she got up early and went to the book without first washing, without first eating, weak from excitement and lack of sleep.

All around, in disorder, on the bed, at the foot of the bed, on the arm-chair beside the bed, even on the floor, clothes were scattered—a rich white silk dress, flowers, ribbons. On the little table at the head of the bed diamonds, which had been taken off and thrown down, lay glittering. At the foot of the bed, some sort of lace lay in a crumpled heap, and on the white lace, protruding from under the sheet, the tip of a bare foot could be made out; it seemed as though it were carved out of marble, and it was dreadfully still. The prince looked, and he felt that the longer he looked the more still and death-like the room became. Suddenly a fly, awakened from its sleep, started buzzing, and after flying over the bed, settled at the head of it. . . .

She was sitting down, yet she was standing—she was next to Myshkin, an apparition of horror and grief. She thought the murder made sense—tragedy made sense; that was the horror of it. Rogozhin's love, which killed, Myshkin's love, which could not save—they were bound by the same despair. Only hatred was stronger than despair—it sprang from despair; it fed on it. Hatred defied human fate. And yet, Rogozhin's hatred was a need to love. She thought of the Dragon suddenly—thought of the hatred he felt as he raised the stone in his hand—and, for a moment, the spell of the book broke. She read on fast:

. . . when many hours later, the door was opened and people came in, they found the murderer completely unconscious and in a raging fever. The prince was sitting motionless beside him on the cushions, and every time the sick man burst out screaming or began rambling, he hastened to pass his trembling hand gently over his hair and cheeks, as though caressing and soothing him. But he no longer understood the questions he was asked, and did not recognize the people who had come into the room and surrounded him. And if Schneider himself had come from Switzerland now to have a look at his former pupil and patient, remembering the condition in which the prince had sometimes been during the first year of his treatment in Switzerland, he would have given him up with a despairing wave of a hand and would have said, as he did then, "An idiot!"

An idiot! She would give her life for Prince Myshkin! She would die for his love! It was magnificent to realize she was capable of such passionate love, a love that could take over her whole being. That was what love was, and nothing else: to bow down and adore goodness and perfection in another. She understood Prince Myshkin. She loved him so passionately because she understood him completely.

Rogozhin she understood, too, though the love she felt for him was marred by pity. But she did love him. *The Idiot* had made her see that she could love a murderer. Rogozhin suffered, and he was too proud to bow to pain. It was pride that made him kill.

IN THE AFTERNOON, she went to Vera's to pick up the assignments she had missed. It was early and she knew the Koroneous would be in bed, napping. But Vera, like herself, did not take naps, and Anna thought she'd hear her if she knocked on the front door softly. There was no response, however. She went to the back door, hoping it was unlocked.

It was, though the shutters in the kitchen windows were closed tight. It was dark inside, so she had to fumble her way through the room. Going down the long corridor, she could not see ahead of her at all. She wished she knew where the light switch was; she felt like an intruder, having to sneak in like this. If they heard her footsteps, they'd think she was a thief. The palms of her hands began to sweat. They may think I'm the Dragon, she thought. They may have already heard me. She was afraid that the boys might jump out at her and beat her. She was too far into the house to turn back; it was the same risk, going in or out—she might as well get in deeper.

Her heart was beating hard and fast as she opened Vera's door. It wasn't like fear anymore, but inexplicable anxiety: Tremors pulsed through her blood, making her veins feel like nerve endings.

Vera was sitting up on her bed, her back propped up by a pillow, her knees open and bent. She was wearing a velvet vest over a ruffled high-collared blouse and matching pants that reached to just below the knee. Her calves were bare, just shaved, and they gleamed as if there were a warm light under her skin, making the light in the air seem cold and pale. She'd shown no surprise when Anna walked in, as though she'd been expecting her, staring at the door. Now she turned her head to the wall.

"You're going out?" Anna asked.

"Yes."

"Where?"

"It does not concern you, where."

She turned her face from the wall and stared at Anna, her eyes haughty and glazed with anger. Slowly, with covert deliberateness, she slid one leg down flat and lowered the other so that it lay still bent at the knee but with a softer curve.

Anna looked away. She did hear me knock, she thought. If I had any dignity, I would leave. But she couldn't bring herself to leave. She stood in the middle of the room like a crate lowered off a ship and left abandoned on the dock.

"Have you heard of *The Idiot*?" she said.

Vera twisted her mouth in a sneer. "Heard and *seen*," she said, looking Anna in the face.

"You want me to leave?"

Vera got up and sat at her vanity table. She started teasing her hair.

"You want me to leave, say, 'Leave!' "

"Leave."

They looked at each other through the mirror.

"Leave! You heard me say it! Leave!"

Anna started walking out.

"Close my door! Close the goddamn door after you!" Vera shrieked. "You bitch! I waited for you to call all weekend."

Anna walked out. She should have called *me*, she thought. She might have been sick, and Vera hadn't even called to find out. Yet as soon as she was out of the room, she wanted to go back in and apologize. For what? she thought. For what!

She breathed a little easier when she was out on the street, but the anxiety did not leave. The street was empty because of siesta time. The shutters of every house were closed, and the stark white walls seemed to inhale sunlight and breathe out silence while they shone. The only sound one could hear was the shrill whistling of the northern wind. It was fierce when it gusted. Anna had to lean into it for it not to topple her, and the effort made her feel frail and small—a speck that could be swept away and no one would know it was gone.

Suddenly, through tears as though through mist, she noticed the sketch of a man's face pasted around an electric pole. It was handsome—broad, with a high forehead. The hair was thick, parted on the side and long on top, falling over the right eye in a supple upturning wave. Below the sketch, in large block letters, was printed: WANTED; and in smaller, regular print underneath: " 'The Dragon.' Average height, dark eyes and hair, of age between 25 and 30 years."

So the woman had regained consciousness after all. Anna hadn't listened to the radio the last few days. She wiped her eyes and studied the Dragon's picture carefully. His face evoked a sense of immediate, if vague, recognition, the individual features like pieces in a puzzle that had loose, wobbly cracks. It was just his good looks, perhaps. All attractive men evoked that sense, that one knew them from somewhere. He could be any handsome young man walking the street. The sketch artist had given his face no expression. The lips were full, set in a straight, firm line; the eyes large, chiseled like a statue's, the pupils perfectly centered, staring with a sullen, intense, inscrutable gaze.

As she moved away, she noticed that the sketch had been pasted around every tree along the street.

The wind had stopped gusting and blew with a steady sweep. The bare branches quivered as they swayed and their latticed shadow shifted on the sidewalk like a broken grid. As she had been afraid of stepping on flagstone cracks when she was small, she was suddenly afraid to step on the dark slats of shade. She moved to the center of the street.

There was no traffic. The street was deserted. From tree to tree, she stared at the Dragon's face as she was walking, and it was as if he were staring back, the stark intensity of his gaze beginning to seem like loneliness and yearning. She saw him in her mind's eye coming toward her with a slow, way-worn stride, his shoulders sagging, his face sad with solitude, gentle with feeling, beseeching her love—redemption only she could give him.

SUNDAY NIGHT, a new murder victim was discovered. She was a fifteen-year-old girl, killed in an empty lot a block away from her house. It was estimated that the murder had occurred two to three hours after the posters were put up. By Monday morning, the Dragon's face was everywhere one looked: on flyers littering the streets, around telephone poles and trees, on fences, alongside public buildings' entrance gates, below movie house photo cases, on the front pages of newspapers displayed in row after row around vending kiosks. The vagueness of the depicted features gave the drawing an autonomous reality, like something conjured by the imagination of the artist. The ubiquity of the sketch made the man seem unreal but, like a saint's icon, inspired belief in his perpetual existence. Panic was palpable throughout the city.

Anna was oblivious. On her way to school, she had been in agony over having to face Vera; then, when she got there, over the way Vera bluntly and blatantly ignored her. Now, as they sat next to each other at the desk, Vera kept glancing in her direction, but when Anna stared back, she turned her head away after first giving her a withering smile, the more scornful for being faint.

The math teacher, an older, punctilious man who discussed nothing but math and dealt with the class in an impersonal, authoritative manner, started the lesson with a lecture.

"I know you're scared," he said. "But you're all perfectly safe, so long as you don't go out on the streets alone. Make sure there's a man who can protect you always with you. You should keep the front door locked and all window shutters securely closed. If, on your way to or from school, any man stares at you persistently or tries to follow you, you should tell a policeman, even if the man is someone you know."

Teacher after teacher started class by giving them the same lecture. This is a solution? Anna thought. If safety meant they could not walk on the streets alone, if safety meant they should barricade themselves like prisoners in their own homes, if safety meant they should turn snitch and tell on men who stared at them, they'd be better off dead. The only life worth living was a life worth having.

Her indignation hour after hour made her confusion about Vera abate, and toward the end of the day she felt only frustration and rage. But for the first time in her life, the anger ate at her rather than making her feel strong. It was like wanting to lash out with a whip and having no hand to hold the grip—as if her fist were maimed.

By the time composition class started, she was so upset, she no longer cared if her paper was read out. She had been thrilled with it last night, however. She had always been praised for her writing, and the praise usually made her feel caught red-handed, carrying a prize to which she had no right. Bad writing was her doing, but good writing came out that way on its own, she thought, and it was like playing it false to claim credit. This time, she felt she had owned the words; she'd thought hard over them—she'd labored and earned them. She'd been proud.

Prokopiou entered the class, looking as if she'd been up all night. The skin on her face was ashen and flaccid, and there were purple blotches under her eyes. She collected the assignments, set them in a tall pile, and clasped her hands, resting her forearms flat on the desk. In turn, her lips quaked and pulled tight as if she were mulling over some distasteful thought.

"You shouldn't let the recent events affect you," she said at last. "The fiercer the storm, the steadier the sailor keeps his hand on the tiller. Panic makes disaster strike twice."

The class was quiet; the silence seemed to weigh on and clutter the air. Prokopiou paused, then picked a paper from the pile and called out the student's name.

Anna got the gist of what the girl had written: The Dragon was a monster; the metaphor in the image his name suggested captured his inner nature; he was abominable; he was evil; he had no conscience or soul. She was too riled up to pay full attention. Composition after composition seemed to go down the exact same course of thought. It was a matter of waiting for time to pass. She kept looking at the clock.

With five minutes remaining to the period and the second hand on the clock steadily shifting, Prokopiou reached into the pile and picked out another composition.

"One last one," she said. "Ah, Karystinou—good."

Anna was shaken up. "Do we have time?"

"Read till the bell rings," Prokopiou said. "And hurry."

Anna began:

"A dragon is a creature that looks like a huge lizard. Its head has a long snout with teeth like a crocodile, but its body sits higher on the legs and has a wider girth. It has scaly, impenetrable skin. It breathes fire but is cold-blooded, like a serpent.

"Dragons are imaginary beasts. In fairy tales and ancient myths, they serve the designs of an evil or enemy king. They have brute force and guile, but they are not evil in themselves. They obey the will of their master and, as mentioned above, serve his cause. In the end, they're killed by the hero of the myth, who is invariably the crown prince of a rival kingdom.

"Trying to analyze how the word *dragon* applies as metaphor for the killer, I was foiled by four things: the fact that in reality dragons do not exist; the fact that they are invincible to common men; the fact that they are repulsive; the fact that they obey their master's command, carrying out their duty when they kill.

"I see a metaphor. But it is a metaphor for what people would *like* to believe. In reverse order: The killer is an instrument of the devil; he's too hideous in appearance and indomitable in strength to be human; he can't really exist.

"It's shocking that grown people can become so besotted with fear that they'd rather deny reality than face the truth it bids. It brings to mind small children who are afraid to go to sleep, believing the shadows in the dark are monsters. Even when we are innocent and trusting, we don't imagine that what is hiding in the dark may be beautiful or benign. It seems to be an innate belief that what we can't see in clear light intends us harm, and that if we come face-to-face with it, it will kill us. What triggers the fear? The hidden knowledge that we're destined to die.

"The killer brings this knowledge out in the open. We call him 'the Dragon' to make him a scapegoat of our fear.

We want him caught and put to death. But he's a man, and we'd be killing a man, not our fear. We hate him because we're not honest enough to hate our fear. We make a monster of him, so as not to face the monstrous cowardice in us.

"We can't be men till we've looked death in the eye.

"We call the killer 'evil.' What of the killer in us?

"Christ said, 'Resist not evil.' What of the evil in us?

"The Dragon does not resist the evil in himself.

"The Dragon obeys his destiny, like a tragic hero standing up to the horror and solitary magnitude of his fate. He's all too human—he's all too real.

"To hate him is to hate every man.

"To fear him is to fear every man.

"If we see him with love in our hearts, we'll see he's no different from us and that when he kills, it's a desperate act, a crying out for love."

She looked up. Prokopiou coughed as though to clear her throat before giving her comments, but instead of speaking, she stared down at her hands.

"Your next assignment is a free theme," she said after a moment. "Anna, you stay here. The rest of you are dismissed."

The next class was gym. The girls gathered their things to take them to the changing room, so they could leave for home directly. They were slow about it, silent.

"Ideas can be like matches in the hands of a child," Prokopiou said when everyone was gone. "You can't just play with them. When you make a case, you have to prove it—with references, with quotes. Ideas do not stand without foundation in proven knowledge. Your arguments were all wrong.

"I'm not going to give you a grade. I want you to think

hard about what I said. It does not only apply to your writing, but to the way you think and speak." She tapped the sides of the papers to even them up, picked them up, and put them in her briefcase. "Go," she said, without looking at Anna. "You'll be late for your next class."

Anna started gathering her things. If my arguments were wrong, why didn't she counter them? she thought. No one else used references or quotes, and she let it go. What was Anna supposed to surmise—that platitudes were freestanding ideas but that original thought had to bow and scrape to canonized thought for support? There was nothing wrong with the way she spoke. She said what was on her mind and did not mince words. From now on, she'd keep her thoughts to herself—she wouldn't say a word of what she really thought.

Everyone, everything, is against me, she thought. Everyone, everything, wants to crush me.

BY THE TIME she got down to the basement, gym class had already started. She could hear the girls marching around the yard, Trita's whistle—each blow tearing the air like a shrill, short-winded scream. The changing room was long and narrow, with no windows and two doors opposite each other, one leading into the building and the other out to the yard. When she'd shut the inner door behind her, the draft had pulled the door to the yard toward the jamb, and it was creaking at the hinges. She didn't want to shut it all the way for fear of being sealed in, didn't want to open it for fear of being seen. She thought that if she waited out the class, no one would know she wasn't in the ranks.

Time dragged. The room was musty and dark. Two of the fluorescent light rods were burned out and the third was flickering. The intermittent flaring glare was like a splinter being wedged in and out of her brain, but she kept her eyes open. She didn't care.

When the class was over and the girls started filing in, every girl staring at her askance and going around her as though she were a hurdle, she didn't care. When Vera sat down next to her, with the bench farther down empty, she didn't care. She got up off the bench.

"Could I borrow your comb?" Vera asked.

She moved away, though her heart skipped a beat when she heard Vera speak.

"I don't carry a comb. As you well know."

She stood five feet away from Vera, wanting to leave but unable to find the will to move. She doesn't care about me, she thought. She felt as if she were about to break down and cry, but she didn't care. She didn't care about anything. She didn't care.

"I have to leave early," the custodian shouted from behind the door that led to the yard. "I'm locking up!"

"Someone open the other door. We'll suffocate in here."

I'll get the door on my way out, Anna thought. But she didn't move.

Suddenly, the last remaining light went dark. It was pitch-black. There was wild hysteria all around. Someone screamed, "The Dragon! The Dragon!"

Anna thought she was going to be trampled. She could not see who was shoving her, who was grabbing at her, the nails digging in. Everyone was trying to get to the doors. Both doors opened in, she realized. Storming them was blocking the way out for good. There was little space to maneuver, but she was able to extricate herself and stand against the wall. It was like watching a fire soar out of control—standing at the edge of it. More and more girls were screaming, "The Dragon! Help! The Dragon!"

Over the roar, Anna could hear from the yard the voices of Trita, the custodian, and, in a moment, Athanasiades, shrieking, urging the girls to back off. She pushed against the damp wall, her back shivering. She felt a sour taste on her tongue. She wasn't frightened; her stomach was upset and she was cold.

She could hear from far off the siren wails of police cars coming to the rescue. She didn't experience relief.

She did not care.

MORE THAN a dozen policemen came in. They moved single file, weapons drawn, making their way through clusters of half-naked girls—some only in bras and underpants, some in sheer slips, the skin on their faces, shoulders, and arms gouged, dripping blood. A shaft of light came through the rammed yard door, but the far end of the changing room, near the door that opened into the building, was dark and still mobbed.

"Move back! Move back! Out of the way!" a police captain commanded.

He had walked in last and was now pushing his way to the front, asserting his rank. The girls who had been standing near the door scattered toward the benches, revealing behind them, in plain sight, two bodies lying motionless, facedown on the floor. The policeman bent over them, leaning his arm against the wall.

"Call an ambulance," he said quietly.

He knelt by them. As he turned one body over, then the other, the legs swiveled and thudded on the floor. In the dim, dust-speckled light, their faces were eerily still and soft. Anna could see that it was Evangelia and Christina, yet it was like looking at two strangers' faces: Evangelia's squashed and swollen, covered with gray bruises and caked blood; Christina's without marks, her eyes rolled back, showing only the whites, a thin stream of blood winding down from her mouth to her chin.

"What happened?" the captain said. "Will someone tell me?"

Everyone turned away from the side of the room where the bodies lay.

"The light went out," Anna said.

"Who turned it off?"

"No one. It burned out. It was pitch-black, and everyone panicked, and someone screamed, 'The Dragon!' and everyone pushed for the door."

"Is that true?"

A few girls nodded silently.

The policeman went out into the yard, motioning to his men to follow. "You all wait in here!" he said to the girls.

The policemen walked out with stiff, hurried steps. Slowly, the girls began to dress.

In a few moments, two ambulance attendants came in and removed the bodies on stretchers.

Vera nudged Anna softly on the arm. "Do you think they are dead?" she whispered.

"They're dead," Anna said.

"The policeman would have said something if they were dead."

"They're dead. You saw them."

"The policeman would have said something," Vera said again.

"Don't you think the ambulance would have turned its siren on and left already? They're dead. I'm telling you, they're dead!"

Vera started to weep, her body shaking with quiet sobs, her arms limp at her sides.

Anna wanted to flee. If she stood still one moment longer, she'd fall apart. She had to run. She couldn't breathe.

"I have to go."

"He said to wait," Vera said through sobs.

"I have to go!" Her voice was shaking. "I have to go!"

She ran frantically toward the yard, then backtracked. The police would stop her if she went that way. She had to go through the corridor door, bypassing the area where Evangelia's and Christina's bodies had lain. It was like skirting an invisible pit. If she stepped too close, she'd fall in, damning her soul. She was trembling when she was out in the corridor.

The building was empty, the gate ajar, the custodian missing from his post. She slipped out unnoticed.

Out on the street, her anxiety focused on which way to go. She walked halfway down the block, then stopped. The back road, she thought. No, by the seashore. She was paralyzed. She looked right, then left. Sitting at the only occupied table of the sidewalk café a couple of yards away, two men were playing checkers. They looked up, stared at her curiously a moment, then went back to their game.

"I give you five to one the Dragon is going to strike again next Sunday," the waiter said. He rested his hand absently on the awning winch.

"A ten spot," one of the men said. "You're on."

"Change the damn station. I've had it, listening to the same news all day," the other man said.

The waiter flicked a speck of lint off his apron and went inside the store. Anna could hear the screeching static as he changed the station, then the slow waltz tune of a song she remembered from her childhood.

Let your hair loose
Let it tangle in the mad wind

It's spring
Everything's in bloom
Let your hair down
Let your hair loose

The sun was shining in an empty bright blue sky. A small bird flew over her head, lighted on a table, and began to chirp. She decided to take the back way, past the café—past the music.

Wanting to be at some distance from the men, she got off the sidewalk and walked in the street. Life seemed to have closed over Evangelia's and Christina's deaths like water over a sinking stone. She was lost in thought. As she went around the curve, a car, coming fast from behind, nearly hit her. Shocked, unable to move, she watched it swerve and slow down. In the backseat, riding backward, was a little girl with hair in pigtails and long, wispy bangs. She saw Anna watching her and smiled a gap-toothed smile. Then, pressing her face against the rear window, she stared back, her features hideously flattened.

Two Days in June

THE ACADEMIC YEAR at the War College was over. Stephanos had received his new orders, a transfer to a base in the apex between the Turkish and Bulgarian border. The move was to be in three days. Except for the beds, the kitchen table, and four chairs, the contents of the house had been packed in wooden crates that lay stacked on the living room floor.

It was early evening. Aimilia had spent the day overseeing the soldiers who did the packing. She had not had to lift a finger; nevertheless, she was exhausted. It is the emotional drain, she thought. With every move, the furniture went into the crates more battered and worn, the packing straw seeming as futile as dressing on a fatal wound. She had been furious at the soldiers' clumsiness and rough handling. She had a houseful of good things in Athens in storage—precious, invaluable things from her parents' estate—yet these ramshackle things seemed like all she'd ever live with.

When Stephanos had refused her dowry, she had been at first appalled, but she had come to see his point: You do not display a diamond in a cardboard box. But another point, too, was beginning to dawn on her: Put the diamond in a vault, all you have to show for life is the box. The feast lay on the table and they were scrambling on their knees to feed on the scraps that had fallen off.

I believe because it is absurd. . . . They were going to the circus tonight.

She went out to the front porch, to wait outside. Maritsa was standing on the landing, leaning against the balustrade, wearing only shorts and a thin shirt.

"Go get a jacket to take along," she told her daughter. "It may get cold. And tell your father I'm out here, waiting already."

"Will there be elephants in the circus?" Maritsa asked when she came back.

"Yes."

"Will there be lions?"

"Yes."

"Will there be monkeys?"

"Yes. It's the third time you asked."

Maritsa bent her head. She went and sat on the top step of the stairs, elbows on knees, chin in cupped hands.

"Don't sit like that. You've been told."

Anna came out, Stephanos a step behind her, buttoning his shirt.

"All set," he said.

Aimilia gave him a withering look. Follow the leader. Let the trumpets blare.

She marched down the steps ahead of him, but he caught up and took hold of her arm, reaching out to Maritsa with his free hand, leaving Anna to walk by herself behind.

"I thought we'd have the new car," Aimilia said.

"So did I. Tomorrow."

"I'll see it and I'll believe it. It's been 'tomorrow' for a week. The moving van will come and we'll still be waiting for the car."

Stephanos put a cigarette in his mouth.

"You should have kept the old car till the new one was delivered."

"Should have. You always know the *should have*."

He lit the cigarette, but the bus came around the corner and he had to put it out. He squashed the butt with the tip of his shoe, staying behind a moment, then overtook them as they ran toward the bus.

It was an old bus, in bad repair. As it went over potholes or around curves, it rattled, shaking like a luffing sail. The driver drove recklessly, much too fast. Stephanos put a new cigarette in his mouth and let it dangle from his lips unlit. He sat up rigidly, gripping his knees.

Aimilia glanced at him, then looked out the window. She wanted to laugh. Were he at the wheel, he'd go as fast. There, she thought, you see the man. Small taste of his own medicine, and he cannot take it.

Two stops before the stop at which they were supposed to get off, he reached above the seat and pulled the cord.

"We're getting off," he said.

The bus hurled to a stop and they rushed to get off.

"I left my shoe up on the bus," Anna said.

"Left it!" Aimilia said. "What do you mean, *left* it?"

"It slipped off as I came down the steps. The door closed."

"Why didn't you signal to the driver to stop?"

"I don't know."

Stephanos took uninterrupted staccato puffs on his cigarette without taking it out of his mouth. He stared at Anna's bare foot but said nothing.

"Those were brand-new sandals," Aimilia said. "I don't know what to say to you."

They started to walk down the street, Anna limping along. People turned their heads to stare.

"We should be *in* the circus," Aimilia said. "A freak show. We should all take one shoe off and walk."

She bent over, laughing hysterically.

"Oh my God! Oh my God!" she said, crossing herself. "I must be losing my mind."

The center of town looked like a city under siege. There were policemen on every corner and armed soldiers patrolling the streets. After a two-month hiatus, the killings had resumed.

Aimilia sobbed softly, feeling the edge of hysteria give way. They were coming close to the park. The circus tent was at the far end, bright red in the shadow of dusk.

"Who was it in mythology—the hero who lost his sandal?" Stephanos asked.

"Jason," Aimilia told him.

"That's right, Jason. Hey, Anna," he said in a cajoling voice. "Remember Jason? History repeats itself. We have the dragon; we have the one-sandaled youth in you. We're missing the Golden Fleece. I was never sure what the Golden Fleece was meant to be, anyway."

"It was a pelt," Anna said, without looking at him.

" 'It was a pelt,' " Aimilia said, mimicking Anna's voice. "It was the fleece of the winged ram that flew Phrixus and Helle over the Hellespont."

"So, it was a pelt," Anna said.

She had been walking a step ahead. Abruptly, she pushed forward at a faster pace, limping furiously on her bare foot. They had entered the park, and clearly the pebbled path caused her pain, but instead of stepping more softly, she gave her limp a harder thrust.

Stephanos watched her, for a moment looking as if he were about to yell at her to stop it, but his mouth went slack. He breathed shallowly and, as he reached into his pants pocket for his cigarette pack, Aimilia could see that his hand was trembling.

"Call her back," he said. "She'll lose us in the crowd."

"She'll wait by the gate."

He looked unsure. There was an urgency to the way he hastened his pace.

"She scampered like a wounded animal," he said.

Aimilia touched his arm. Stronger than passion, stronger than affection, this part of her love for him remained: She knew his pain.

"Well now," she said, as they approached the entrance to the tent, "there she is."

Anna was standing by the entrance, across from the ticket taker, her bare foot on tiptoe, her arms behind her back. There was a tear on her jeans over the right knee, but her blouse was brand-new—a gaudy affair in shiny blue rayon with a crimson flower print that she'd made Aimilia buy for her as a birthday gift.

"All I can say is, you'd better have gotten us numbered seats," she told her father. "It's mobbed in there."

She walked inside ahead of them.

"First row—ring seats," Stephanos called after her.

She didn't turn her head to look back at him. When they were down at the pit, Aimilia whispered in her ear, "It was a sacrifice for him to get good seats. Do you know how much they cost? Thank him!"

Anna grabbed the ticket stub from her hand and read it.

"I'm going to sit down."

Stephanos and Maritsa went to get peanuts.

Aimilia followed Anna into the seats, enraged. It had become impossible to talk to her anymore—impossible to deal with her without wanting to grab her shoulders and shake her. When she was not hiding her face behind a book, she lay about like a caged animal. She let her hair congeal with grease, did not change her clothes till they were soiled and rank, talked back in a shrill, contentious voice or responded with a neighing, mirthless laugh. Despite the lithe, graceful contours of her body, she moved like a mule pulling a cart, and she sat with her legs sprawled and her back slumped.

"Thank him when he comes back," she told Anna again.

"Since when are you taking his side?"

"His side! How am I taking his side? It's you I'm concerned about—how you behave. When someone is nice to you, you should thank them."

"I'll remember that."

Stephanos and Maritsa came back.

"Why is that man holding an electric cord?" Maritsa asked.

"That man is called the MC and that's a microphone cord," Stephanos explained. "See that thing he has in his hand? It will make his voice come out loud when he starts to speak."

He had sat Maritsa next to him, between Aimilia and himself. They had center seats, caught in the sharp periphery of the spotlight. It looks like we're part of the show, Aimilia thought. There were no other spectators in their row.

Maritsa ignored the clowns who had started warming up

the crowd, keeping her eyes on the microphone cord. During the opening parade, with horses in feathers and glimmering tassels, elephants with sequined saddles, monkeys dressed in human clothes, acrobats with rhinestone-studded tights, she still seemed to be thinking of the cord.

"It was so long, Daddy," she said. "It was long like a water hose."

Aimilia tried to watch the show but could not take in what she saw. She'd seen it all before. Seen the circus. Seen her life. Now, for the new, repeating act . . .

"Ladies and gentlemen!" the MC announced. "Our show's main attraction! Gudrun, Germany's greatest living legend, will perform the *salto mortale*, 'the leap of death'—a triple somersault through the air, without a net."

There was a long drumroll while stagehands took down the net. A hush had fallen over the crowd.

"Ladies and gentlemen, Gudrun the Great!"

The aerialist stepped to the end of the raised platform, waved her arm in salute, and reached for the swing. She had a compact, muscular body with thickset thighs and a stern face framed by short black hair cut like a sleek helmet. For all the vigor of her young body, she had a dissipated look—hardened, embittered lines around a sensual mouth, and a sickly pallor, deep hollow circles under the eyes. Aimilia was repulsed.

"Ladies and gentlemen! I beseech your silence."

There was a slow drumroll. The aerialist swung on the trapeze one time, two times, three, four—Aimilia, finding herself caught in suspense, was enraged. Her nerves were ready to snap as it was; the last thing she needed was to be wrung with tension over some stupid trapeze act. Jump already! she thought. She couldn't stand the woman.

The drum stopped beating at last. The aerialist tore through the air, tumbling only once.

Anna stood on her feet and started clapping wildly in the ensuing hush, yelling, "Bravo! Bravo!"

Aimilia pulled on her blouse to force her down.

"You're making a spectacle of yourself. No one else is applauding."

Anna continued to clap and yell.

"Sit down. You're acting like a fool."

"I don't care."

Aimilia looked in Stephanos's direction for support, but Stephanos would not meet her eyes.

"Didn't you see she aborted the act?"

Anna sat down at last.

"She jumped without a net. She risked her life." Her face was flushed and she was breathing fast. "She was the only one to do her act without a net." She leaned over Aimilia's seat to get her father's attention. "None of the men took the chance. None of the men! She was not afraid to risk her life. That is the greatest heroism known to man—and a woman has done it!"

"One does not applaud the risk," Stephanos said. "One applauds success. Any fool can take a risk."

"A fool does not take a risk *knowingly*. That's what makes him a fool," she answered. "She took the risk knowingly, which is brave. It's courage, not success, that should be applauded. To leap through the fear of death, while people watch, is to leap for everyone—is to leap through the fear of the whole world."

Stephanos lowered his eyes.

"You're speaking too loudly," Aimilia said. "Not everyone wants to hear what you have to say."

"I want them to hear. They can go to hell if they don't want to hear."

She turned her face away from Aimilia and looked, enraptured, at center stage, where the aerialist was taking her bow. Aimilia stared at her. Of all the idols she could find. The lofty fervor on Anna's face, the lovelorn adoration in her eyes made her despair. They were beyond adolescent idealism and yearning. She'd always had fire in her and no sense of bounds. She burned her bridges, did not mark her exits, took the untrodden path with the deluded confidence of a gambler trusting his luck. God knew what was to become of her.

The final parade had started. Performers and animals were marching together in a slow, out-of-step procession to the tune of "Semper Fidelis." Aimilia gazed at the animals as they went by, sullen and supple with forbearance. They seemed to have a full understanding of their fate. The men who led them walked with a pompous, blind stare, a stiff-backed stride.

WHEN ANNA GOT UP the next morning, the house was quiet and dark. The beds in her parents' and Maritsa's rooms were empty. Aimilia, in a backless white beach dress, was making sandwiches in the kitchen.

"Where is everybody?"

"Everybody had his new car delivered at six this morning. He's gone to the bus depot to get your sandal. Bring me the other one. I want to see if we can't punch a hole and make the strap a little tighter."

"I don't have it."

Aimilia wrapped the sandwich she had made in wax paper and put it in the picnic basket by her feet.

"Don't have it? What do you mean, you don't have it?"

"I put it in a waste bin at the circus."

Aimilia's face contorted with anger, but she stayed silent.

"I didn't think we could get the other one back," Anna said.

"You didn't think! You can't be impetuous—do you understand me? You threw out a perfectly good sandal."

Anna felt falsely accused. She had acted with weighed conviction: However perfectly good, perfectly useless made a thing onerous to keep. She'd given the sandal she'd lost no thought. Lost, so be it. One should walk away from what was broken. Mending only covered up the fault.

She put some milk in a saucepan and set it on the stove.

"We're out of cocoa," she said, opening the cupboard.

"We're leaving in two days. Have it plain."

Anna turned the stove off and poured the milk back in the bottle. It made her gag, plain hot milk.

"I had a bad dream," she said. "I was sailing in a brig with red sails. There was no one at the wheel, no one else on board. I was completely alone. I couldn't see the shore. I looked up and realized that the red color on the sails was blood."

"Was the water clear?"

"It was clear."

"It's a good dream," Aimilia said. "Water is good. Red is good."

"It was blood."

Aimilia did not say anything to that. She lowered her eyes and cut another slice of bread. "Go pack your swimsuit and pajamas," she said after a moment.

"My pajamas?"

"We're going to Chalkidiki, to inaugurate the car."

"It's my class party tonight."

Aimilia went on making sandwiches.

"Did you hear me? It's my class party tonight. You knew it was. You don't care what *I* want to do. You never ask me. You—"

She heard the front door open. She'd have to buck up and tell Stephanos she'd thrown her sandal away.

But when he came into the kitchen, he left a shoe-size newspaper-wrapped packet on the counter and made no reference to it.

"Ready yet?" he said.

"I'm staying home," she told him. "It's my class party tonight and I want to go."

"You be back by nine," Stephanos said. "When I say nine, I mean nine." He turned to Aimilia. "I'll be waiting outside."

Anna followed after him to see the new car.

"Is that a car, or is that a car?" he said as they went through the gate.

"It's a sports car!"

He laughed.

Anna had never heard him laugh with such full joy before. She circled the car, hoping she could warm up to it. It was white, low to the ground, with a long front like a swollen duckbill, a solid squat roof, and almost no trunk. The backseat was narrow, with barely any legroom, and had no stuffing. Maritsa looked squashed sitting in it.

Stephanos put the overnight suitcase and the straw mats for the beach next to Maritsa in back and got in the front seat.

"Nine o'clock!" he said, sticking his head out the window. "Go get your mother."

But Aimilia was already at the gate.

"Call the Marketous if anything goes wrong," she said as she got in the car. "Call them right away and tell them you'll be in the house alone."

The engine made a deafening roar; the car sped off, hugging the road as though it were rolling in a groove. The old car had had a whine, a hesitancy like regret as it chugged on. This one was conquer and forsake. It took her breath away.

She went back upstairs and sat on a crate in the corner of the living room. There was nothing to do. The party wasn't till six in the evening. She picked up the phone from the floor and dialed Vera's number, hoping she would answer the phone, but it was Dr. Koroneou who picked up. He asked her curtly to wait.

She was a long time on hold.

"You woke me up," Vera said.

"What time are we meeting?"

"Five-thirty. Didn't we say five-thirty?" She yawned. "What are you wearing?"

"Shorts."

"Not now, you idiot! For the party."

"A knit dress I have."

"What color?"

"Pink."

"I don't see you in pink."

"It's dark pink—between cyclamen and purple."

"Dark pink, maybe . . ."

"What are *you* wearing?"

"My pink-and-red polka-dot dress."

"We'll clash."

"No we won't," Vera said, yawning again. "We'll look outré."

Anna wanted to ask if she could go over. But she wanted to too desperately—it would be like begging.

"Are you there?" Vera said.

Anna let the silence sink in a brief moment.

"Till five-thirty," she said, hanging up.

She went to the kitchen and ate a whole box of cream-filled cookies, stuffing them into her mouth with the palm of her hand. She felt queasy from the sweetness and wished she could throw up.

Next year, Vera would have a new friend. It was always like this with the friends she made. The same life they had had before, they had again, as though Anna were no more than a stray dog they'd fed and chased out of the way. She'd never be able to get used to the hurt. Each time she thought it had been the worst; then it proved there was a hollow, boundless place where next time the pain went in deeper. Well, it would never happen again. She would never, ever again let herself need a friend.

Her eyes fell on her sandal. She picked it up from the counter where Stephanos had left it, unwrapped it, and held it in her hand—a single useless shoe, unthwartable, like a dictate of fate. Clearly, she was meant to own it. Clearly, she was meant to keep it—a keepsake to make her feel lame.

VERA WAS WAITING in front of her house, leaning against a lamppost with her arms behind her back, one leg slightly forward and raised at the ankle, heel off the ground. She was wearing thick red lipstick and rouge, but her dress, of gauzy muslin, looked ethereal. When Anna had put on her dress, it had been like pulling a tight sock down her neck.

The mirror had been packed; all she'd had to go by was the memory of how the dress had looked on her last year.

As she approached, Vera twirled around the lamppost, unfurling her skirt.

"Voilà."

Anna did not say anything.

"Do you know what a veronica is?" Vera asked her.

"A *Veronica?*"

Vera twirled again. "It is," she said, without letting go of the lamppost, furling and unfurling her skirt with her free hand, "the moment when the matador holds still and flaunts his cape at the bull. Otherwise known as 'the moment of truth.' "

"Well, *my* name has no meaning," Anna said.

"Yes it does. I looked it up. It's Hebrew and it means 'grace.' 'Truth' and 'grace'—how about that?"

"Yeah, how about that?" Anna said. "Shall we go?"

They walked silently toward the shore drive. It was sweltering. When they got to the sea, the water gleamed like glass.

Vera sat down on a bench.

"We don't want to be early," she said, looking at her watch.

"We are on time."

"On time is early."

The promenade was deserted, except for a young mother pushing a pram. A small girl followed close behind, a pinwheel in her hand, her elbow extended as if she were carrying a pennant.

"I used to have a pinwheel," Anna said.

"Everyone used to have a pinwheel."

Anna tried to remember what had happened to her

pinwheel. She couldn't remember how any of her toys had disappeared.

"When I was little, I thought fish lay down on the bottom of the sea to sleep," Vera said. "I thought animals in China had slanted eyes, and that the dead took their coffins with them up to heaven."

"I thought rabbits laid eggs—because of the Easter bunny."

Vera laughed. After a moment, she moved closer. "You know what you want to be?"

"I just decided. Last night."

"Oh?"

"I'm going to be a trapeze artist."

Vera raised her eyebrows.

"I am," Anna said. "You'll see."

"Right."

"You don't want to believe me." The sarcasm in Vera's voice angered Anna so much that she trembled. "You don't want to believe anything I say."

"Want to!" Vera said. "You speak nonsense. A trapeze artist, really!" She got off the bench and started to walk along the boardwalk.

Anna followed two steps behind.

"What's the address?" Vera said, without turning her head to look back at Anna.

"I don't have the address. I thought you'd have it."

Vera turned around.

"You picked me up; you should have the address."

"Like hell I *should*!"

They glared in silence at each other.

"It's one hundred and twenty something," Vera said finally. "It's supposed to be next to a construction site."

They looked across the street.

"Over there," Anna said.

There was a 123 and a 125 address on either side of the construction site. Anna looked at the names on the bells of 123.

"Lydia has a stepfather," Vera told her. "Her name wouldn't be on the bell."

"I have a feeling it's the other building."

"A . . . *feeling*? You have a feeling? What do you aim to do—ring all the bells?"

"It's the penthouse."

They walked over to the next building. "What if it's the wrong place?" Vera said as they were going up on the elevator.

"I told you, I have a feeling."

They rang the bell. A uniformed maid opened the door, looked them over, and, without motioning them in, walked away, toward the back of the apartment.

After a moment's hesitation, they stepped into the hall. The apartment was totally quiet, the living room empty.

"Now what?"

"It's here," Anna said. "I have a feeling. Besides, the maid would have asked who we were if it wasn't the right place."

She went into the living room and sat down on the sofa. Vera followed her but remained standing.

"You're crazy. You know that."

"We should go out to the veranda."

"Yeah, and jump off!"

"The party is out there. I have a feeling."

"Your heart brimmeth over this evening."

The door to the veranda was open. When they got closer,

they could see several of their classmates sitting in a semi-circle on folding chairs, heads bent. They were completely silent and still, woebegone expressions on their faces.

Vera doubled over, laughing hysterically.

"I'm d-d-dreaming this," she stammered. "It's a n-n-nightmare."

They walked out and sat on the two empty seats, at the end of the circle.

"We're observing half an hour's silence for Evangelia's and Christina's deaths," the girl sitting next to them whispered.

Vera covered her face with her hands. Anna was no longer sure if Vera was laughing or weeping. She watched her uncomfortably. After a moment, Anna stood up. It was hard to sit still.

At last, Lydia looked at her watch.

"Life to us!" she said.

"Life to us!" the girls said like a chorus.

Lydia put the Platters' "Only You" on the gramophone and sat down again.

"Were you laughing or crying?" Anna asked Vera in a whisper.

"L-l-laughing." She covered her face up again. "Oh my God . . . Oh my God . . . I can't stop. D-d-dance with me! Do something!"

She got up teetering on her legs and flung her arms around Anna's neck. She clung to her. Anna tried to move to the music, but the pulsing tremor in Vera's body was paralyzing. She held her tightly—with sudden, unbearable grief. Vera pulled back. Her face was flushed, her eyes dilated and stark, as when one stares out of the dark depth of sobbing laughter. Her body quieted. She blinked—slowly, like a cat in the sun.

"I love this song," she said.

Anna pulled Vera back close to her and hid her face in Vera's shoulder. She was afraid she'd start crying. She was amazed at how soft Vera's bones felt, how light she was to hold, as if she were hollow, a bundle of reeds—Anna's love slipping through them like wind. She felt lonelier than when their bodies did not touch. It was not enough to touch. She did not know what would be enough. She wanted to tear into her. She wanted to squeeze so hard, she'd feel something solid, real.

The music was now "The Great Pretender." It was her favorite Platters' song. She understood all but a few of the words.

> *Oh yes, I'm the great pretender*
> *Pretending that I'm doing well*
> *My need is such*
> *I pretend too much*
> *I'm lonely but no one can tell*
>
> *Oh yes, I'm the great pretender*
> *Adrift in a world of my own . . .*
> *Too real is this feeling of make believe*
> *Too real what I feel*
> *What my heart can't conceal*

"That's how you lead," Vera said, lowering Anna's right arm and pressing it into the small of her back. "What's the matter? You're trembling."

"There's something I have to tell you," Anna said.

She realized as they pulled apart that they were the only ones dancing. Everyone was staring at them.

"I'm going to leave—Thessaloniki—forever. My father got his transfer."

"When?"

"This Monday."

"The day after tomorrow?"

"In two days, yes."

"How long have you known?" Vera shrieked.

"Vera, they're staring at us."

"How long have you *known*?"

"Three weeks—about. I didn't tell you—it was too upsetting to tell you."

" 'Too upsetting to tell me'? Too upsetting to tell me!" Vera screamed. "You scum! You two-faced scum!" She grabbed Anna by the shoulders and hit her against the wall. "You snake! You—" Her face became calm. "You know what?" she said in a low, flat voice. "You're twisted. You think you're so smart, you think you're so high-and-mighty, but you're twisted—*twisted*! That's all you are—TWISTED!" She had started to shout again. "Like your handwriting, you are. It looks beautiful and clear, but you look close enough and you can't read a word. Every single letter is hideous, it's so warped."

The record had come to an end, and the needle screeched in the empty grooves. Anna waited for someone to lift it, but no one was making a move. The girls stood as though frozen, staring at her with mean, haughty expressions on their faces, identical to the one on Vera's. She did not think the moment would end.

"So you should know," Vera said, coming closer to whisper in Anna's ear. "Your dress shows the crack in your ass."

She walked over to the gramophone, changed the record to "My Prayer," and asked Lydia, whom she said she despised, to dance.

The girls looked away from Anna and started to act as though she were no longer there. She couldn't move for a few moments. She watched Vera and Lydia dance, feeling her heart tighten. She felt no pain in it, but a jolting continuous spasm that sent waves of anxiety and shame through her. She would never be able to hold her head up again.

It was hard to walk. Her body weighed her down, and the effort it took to move made her fear she'd faint. But when she was outside the apartment, in the hall, waiting for the elevator, she couldn't stand still. She took the stairs, seven flights down, her strength returning as she descended.

Out on the street she walked fast—so fast, it was as if she were soaring on the impetus of her motion. Her breathing had slowed down. It was as if she could walk this way forever and put the anxiety aside. She was afraid to stop. She would fall apart if she stopped. She would lose her mind if she stopped.

She walked along the shore, not looking around her, not caring where the road led. She'd keep walking till her body had no more will, she decided. But when that did happen, when her body felt like a rag, it was still terrifying to stop. I'll go to the end of the road, she thought. I have to go to the end of the road.

SHE WALKED for hours, clear to the outskirts of town. The road ended at a small cove. Pine woods, covering the land fork, hid the city from view. In a clearing at the lip of the water was a wrought-iron bench and a solitary lamppost. It was nightfall, but the light was still soft. There was a slight, almost imperceptible breeze, and the surface of the sea rippled, curling like a lamb's gentle fleece.

Her feet hurt terribly; she had to take her shoes off. She climbed on the bench, then onto the top slat of the back rest and started to walk on it back and forth, balancing with outstretched arms. She did not know what made her do it. I can jump, she thought. If I jump, I won't fall off. She took a high hop and landed squarely back on the top slat. She felt a joy so serene, it was as though her heart had stopped beating. I *will* be a trapeze artist, she thought. I can do anything I want. I can do anything I please.

She didn't want to move—didn't want to upset the joy—but her eyes unwittingly looked down and she saw, long and motionless on the ground, the shadow of a man—the shape of sharp-angled shoulders, a head in a hat. She turned around slowly, steady on her feet, her heart serene. The man was standing with his legs slightly apart, hands in his pants pockets. His shirt was open at the collar, the sides of his jacket bunched up over his wrists. His suit was white and glimmered in the dark, but his hat was pulled down low and cast a shadow over his face.

He took a cigarette pack out of his pocket, put a cigarette in his mouth, and lit it, cupping his hands over the match. She couldn't see the lower part of his face, but, in the brief moment the flame flared, she saw his eyes—stark with loneliness and rage. He held her glance, then blew out the match. She knew he was the Dragon: Tenderness flooded her heart even as fear welled up. She looked at him with love.

The man puffed on the cigarette, inhaling deeply, and turned quietly on his heels. He walked away toward the pines with a slow, limping gait.

She could hear his retreating footsteps a long time after she was able to see him; then there was silence and, in the silence, she could hear her heart pound fiercely and fast. Fear rushed through her, overpowering her sense of existence. There was nothing else she was aware of, nothing but fear, as though the knowledge that she'd been spared, that she'd have to go on living, were terror. I'm safe, she thought. Intact. But life seemed like something outside of her, air she breathed in and out. There was nothing to hold on to—she had nothing.

She couldn't move. She'd been holding her body so still, it had become numb. She wanted to jump off the bench, but her legs were stiff. To calm herself, she tried to breathe more slowly, more deeply, and, after a while, the fear was gone and feeling came back to her body. She could feel her legs, the soles of her feet—the hard, narrow ledge of the bench cutting into them like a blunt knife. She tried to wiggle her toes. A throbbing, excruciating pain shot up the bottom of her feet, through her body into her mouth. It was as if her teeth were being pulled. Then, in an instant, the pain was gone. She did not feel anything—a strange, total emptiness. She still couldn't move, but she felt light, as though a weight had lifted off, a burden she'd been carrying her whole life. Suddenly, it was as though there were more light—a marvelous brightness all around her. The ground, the trees, the star-filled sky seemed to shine. From the corner of her eye she could see the calm black glimmer of the sea and, far away, long as a ship's wake, shimmering like uncertain hope, a shaft of golden moonlight.

A NOTE ABOUT THE AUTHOR

Irini Spanidou is the author of God's Snake. *She lives in New York City.*

A NOTE ON THE TYPE

*This book was set in Janson, a redrawing of type cast from matrices
long thought to have been made by the Dutchman Anton Janson,
who was a practicing type founder in Leipzig during the years 1668–87.
However, it has been conclusively demonstrated that these types are actually
the work of Nicholas Kis (1650–1702), a Hungarian, who most probably
learned his trade from the master Dutch type founder Dirk Voskens.
The type is an excellent example of the influential and sturdy Dutch types that
prevailed in England up to the time William Caslon developed his own
incomparable designs from them.*

Composed by Creative Graphics, Allentown, Pennsylvania
Printed and bound by Haddon Craftsmen,
an R. R. Donnelley & Sons Company,
Bloomsburg, Pennsylvania
Design by Dorothy Schmiderer Baker